A Place
To Come Back To

A Place
To Come Back To

NANCY BOND

A MARGARET K. MCELDERRY BOOK

Atheneum   *1985*   *New York*

Lines from "The Death of the Hired Man" from *The Poetry of Robert Frost* edited by Edward Connery Lathem reprinted by permission of Holt, Rinehart and Winston Publishers. Copyright 1930, 1939, © 1969 by Holt, Rinehart and Winston. Copyright © 1958 by Robert Frost. Copyright © 1967 by Leslie Frost Ballantine.

Library of Congress Cataloging in Publication Data
Bond, Nancy.
A place to come back to.
"A Margaret K. McElderry book."
Summary: When Charlotte's friend Oliver's life is shattered by the death of his eighty-two-year-old great-uncle and guardian, Oliver turns to Charlotte with urgent demands she finds herself unprepared to meet.
[1. Friendship—Fiction. 2. Death—Fiction]
I. Title
PZ7.B63684Pl   1984   [Fic]   83-48745
ISBN 0-689-50302-4

Published simultaneously in Canada by McClelland & Stewart, Ltd.
Composed by Service Typesetters
Austin, Texas
Manufactured by Fairfield Graphics
Fairfield, Pennsylvania
First Printing March 1984
Second Printing August 1984
Third Printing June 1985

For Heddie and Tack Kent
and Intervale Farm

"Home is the place where, when you have to go there,
They have to take you in."

—Robert Frost
"The Death of the Hired Man"

A Place
To Come Back To

Chapter One

"LOOK OUT!" LOOK OUT!" YELLED DAN SCHUYLER. "GET OUT OF my way!"

"Hey, watch it!" Charlotte exclaimed as he came barreling straight at her through the pale, snowy, January dusk. She stopped hard on her skate tips barely in time to avoid collision, then pushed away on her right blade, down another path. Kath Schuyler swept past, just out of reach, in hot pursuit of her younger brother, making yipping, growling noises, which she felt were appropriate to her role as fox in the game of Fox and Geese they were playing. She had already taggd three geese: Cindy and Carl, the eight-year-old Schuyler twins, and Dougie Williams from one of the houses across the fields. They were huddled together in the little circle of clear ice at the far end of the pond, making rude noises and shouting indiscriminate encouragement to everyone.

It was always sound strategy, in these games, to get the younger, less nimble skaters out of the way of the elders as quickly as possible. Dougie's sister Lynn had only escaped Kath by luck so far—her ankles had begun to fold inward, Charlotte noticed. She wouldn't last much longer. But Kath was intent on Dan and would keep after him until she got him. Charlotte skated gently backward, biding her time, as the fox and the unfortunate goose sped round and round the maze of paths they had shoveled in the new snow.

"You cheat!" yelled Kath, as Dan plowed a desperate shortcut through one of the snow islands.

3

"Help, Andy, help!" he cried, practically running on his skate blades. Andy, who was Kath's twin, skated obligingly in their direction, offering himself as a decoy, but she refused to be distracted.

Off to one side, the other remaining goose, Oliver Shattuck, glided easily, precisely, through the intricate network of paths they had cleared on the ice, apparently oblivious to the chase, but managing, nonetheless, to stay invariably out of range.

Perhaps after this game they should clean the pond altogether and just skate for a while, Charlotte thought, watching him. She suspected he was getting bored with Fox and Geese, and they made a good pair on skates, she and Oliver. Arm-in-arm they could caligraph figures around the others. Andy and Kath, and all the other Schuylers, for that matter, were strong, straightforward skaters, nothing subtle in their style. They had grown up with the pond in their front yard and an uncle, living with them, who had played ice hockey seriously in college until an accident had stiffened his left knee. They loved banging up and down the ice with hockey sticks and an old dog-chewed puck.

Oliver didn't see much in that. He preferred doing clever things on the ice, and he did them well. Charlotte herself couldn't remember learning to skate, she just always had, with her much-older brothers and sister. In the course of fifteen winters she'd become quite good at it. But Oliver had taught himself in the two winters since he came to live with his great-uncle in Concord. Commodore Shattuck gave him a pair of skates as a present his first Christmas, and Oliver, with characteristic determination, had spent hours and hours alone, on a pond off Lowell Road, practicing until he felt he was good enough to let his friends see him. It was as if he were ashamed of having to learn, of not automatically knowing, and it was typical of him. Charlotte had only found out about the practicing by accident from the Commodore one afternoon when she'd gone to see Oliver about something and he wasn't home. Oliver never told her.

Large, feathery flakes of snow sifted slowly out of the sky, seeming to catch and hold the fading gray-pink light. Her eyes on Oliver, Charlotte lost track of what was happening for a few disastrous minutes. Then suddenly she was aware of Lynn and Dan steaming toward her from different directions, scattering snowflakes, Lynn shrieking excitedly, and Kath right behind her. Charlotte dodged Dan again safely and was congratulating herself on her escape, when Andy, head down and not looking, hurtled out of yet another path and knocked her flat. They landed together in an explosion of snow, Andy on top, and before Charlotte could get enough breath back to be indignant, two other bodies crashed around them, falling over Andy's sprawled legs: Lynn and Kath. With a cry of triumph, Dan came swooping back again, meaning to gloat over the tangle, misjudged his footing, and pitched onto the heaving pile himself. The three geese cheered wildly from their pen. Oliver glided smoothly past the heap, deftly avoiding the flailing limbs, and stopped with a flourish.

"As the only one not tagged and still upright, I obviously win," he announced smugly. "Three cheers for me."

Charlotte struggled out of the muddle and sat up. There was snow in her hair, down her neck, and melting on her glasses, which miraculously were still intact though askew. "Without a doubt you are the prize goose," she agreed.

"Who's got my other mitten?" said Andy.

"Get your elbow off my stomach," said Kath.

"Someone deliberately tripped me," declared Dan, rolling off the top. "When I find out who, I'll—"

"So who's fox next?" asked Lynn, emptying snow out of her hat.

"Oliver," said Andy promptly.

"Ow!" yelled Kath. "That's my hand you're kneeling on, you clod!"

"I've won," said Oliver again. "I'm through. It's past four and I'm going home."

"But you can't," protested Andy. "It's much too early to quit. It's not dark yet."

"Doesn't matter, I'm going." Oliver skated toward the railroad tie at the edge of the pond that they used as a bench.

"Hey," Kath called after him, "we could clear the rest of the ice and skate. We don't have to play anymore."

"What do you mean?" said Dan. "Everyone hasn't been

5

fox yet. We can't stop till everyone's been fox."

Oliver sat down and began unlacing a skate, and Charlotte knew he had made up his mind. They could all go on skating, adjust to one person fewer, play Fox and Geese or something else, but his going upset the pattern. It changed things. "My feet are cold," she said loudly, and as if on cue, Andy said, "We could go up to the house for a while—make popcorn and get warm. Then we could come down again later with the lantern. Oliver?"

They looked hopefully in his direction, but he shook his head. "Nope. I can't."

Charlotte refused to beg him to stay; that would make it worse. She got to her feet and cleaned off her glasses.

"*You* don't have to go," Andy said to her. "I can drive you home later, or Dad."

She heaved a sigh, glanced from Oliver working on his second skate to Andy gazing at her beseechingly. "Oh, I'd probably better. I've still got homework."

Andy made a face. Kath got up and dusted herself briskly. "Come on, you guys, let's get the snow shifted and play some hockey." Oliver and Charlotte might already have gone for all the notice she took of them.

"Well," said Andy. "Guess I'll see you in school tomorrow." He sounded wistful.

"Yes," said Charlotte. "Have fun. Hey, Oliver—wait a minute, will you?"

She hurried to catch up with him, fumbled her skates untied, stuck her feet in cold boots, slung the skates over her shoulder, and climbed the long sloping field to the road. He hadn't waited, not until he reached the car. He stood leaning against it, staring out over the darkening countryside. The sound of voices followed her clearly up from the pond, but the figures had merged with the dusk and disappeared.

On both sides of the road lay the Bullard Farm, locked in winter: house, barn, farm stand, fields, and woods, bought nearly a hundred years ago by Andy's grandfather and not much changed since. Except that across the fields shone the lights of houses new since Frank Bullard's day, and beyond the fringe of woods to the south lay a four-lane highway to Boston, usually thick with traffic. And when you looked closely at the barn, which Charlotte knew Andy did all the time, you could see that it bulged ominously on its rear foundation and that its rooftree swayed like the back of an old horse. Andy's father had given up farming when Andy was about nine. George Schuyler was probably, at that moment, out riding a snowplow for the Department of Public Works. He didn't care anymore if the barn fell in, except that it would mean finding another place to store the accumulation of farm junk. Andy cared passionately; Andy meant to spend his life working the farm again.

"Why are you in such a hurry?" asked Charlotte crossly.

Oliver gave a shrug. "I've had enough, that's all. You don't have to leave just because I do, you know."

It was an off-hand, rude sort of answer. He had brought her, after all, and said he'd take her home. But she controlled the urge to point that out, or to mention the fact that Pat Schuyler undoubtedly expected them to come in for cocoa after skating. Pat liked noise and lots of kids surging around. Across the road, the windows of the farmhouse glowed confidently against the cold. Charlotte thought with regret of the cheerful, chaotic warmth inside. Coming as she did from a large, orderly house in which everyone else was much older than she, it had taken her a while to get used to the cluttered, haphazard Schuyler household. She was still glad not to live in it, but she enjoyed visiting. Oliver, she suspected, was less enthusiastic. It was frequently very hard to tell what was going on beneath Oliver's carefully opaque surface; he kept a great deal of himself protected.

There was something going on there now; Charlotte knew it, although she didn't know what. It kept her from arguing with him. In the time they'd been friends, she had learned that it did no good to ask him outright when she thought something was bothering him; it only clamped the lid down tighter. She had to exert patience and wait until he was ready to tell her without being prodded. In silence they climbed in opposite sides of Commodore Shattuck's little blue Ford.

Oliver started the engine, listened thoughtfully as it settled to a steady hum, then put it into gear and eased it onto the road.

The color had leaked from the afternoon. The trees were vertical black charcoal lines against a smoky gray background, sparked here and there by lights. Oliver hunched slightly forward over the wheel, peering ahead with a fixed expression. Whatever was simmering behind that expression had to do with Christmas vacation; Charlotte was sure of that much. He was never eager to visit his mother and stepfather at any time, but this year he hadn't wanted to go to Washington for Christmas at all, he'd made that quite plain. It had done him no good, of course. It was the adults who arranged these things and had the final word.

Charlotte sympathized. Christmas in Concord was lovely, with or without snow, and this year there was some. The Milldam shops glittered with decorations, and the huge living evergreen in the square was garlanded with white lights. The old houses had candles in their windows and wreaths on their doors, and trees sparkled inside, between curtains. There was Christmas Eve caroling in the toe-pinching, cheek-stinging cold, and the Christmas Revels in Cambridge, where everyone sang hard enough to lift the roof off Sanders Theater and the main hall at intermission was packed with the audience, hand-in-hand, dancing in great twisting, jumbled lines. And there were mulled cider and eggnog and cookies and wonderful pies, ribbon candy, chocolate apples. It was a whole, complete, glowing feeling, made up of familiar, well-loved rituals and filled with reliable magic.

She and her father had driven Oliver to the airport in Boston, leaving in ample time to allow for traffic, and still arriving with only minutes to spare. While Mr. Paige stayed with the car, unable to find a place to park it, Charlotte and Oliver raced to the gate, and just before he disappeared through the door, he turned to her, his face intent, and said in a low, urgent voice, "Take care of Uncle Sam." That was all, and he was gone. And Charlotte, standing there, was ambushed by a sudden sharp stab of loss; it caught her quite off-guard. It had nothing to do with feeling sorry for Oliver.

Back in Concord, Mr. Paige complained jokingly that he might as well have been in the car alone for all the company he'd had on the drive home. But Charlotte was too preoccupied to answer back and unwilling to try to explain. She attempted, with some success, to convince herself that the root of her problem was disappointment because her favorite brother, Eliot, was unable to get home from Colorado for Christmas; he was studying coyotes in some inaccessible chunk of the wilderness.

Then, the day after Christmas—Wednesday evening, when they were collapsed around the living room, full of leftovers and lazy with well-being—the telephone rang. "That'll be Eliot," said Mrs. Paige. "Or your brother Douglas," she added with less enthusiasm. "You go, Gordon. I don't think I can bear to hear about their plans for Aruba or St. Thomas this winter." Uncle Doug and Aunt Nell always went somewhere warm in January. Mr. Paige grunted, but didn't move, so with a sigh she went.

But it wasn't Eliot, and it wasn't the Philadelphia Paiges, it was Oliver's mother calling to say he would be returning to Boston the next afternoon, and could she possibly impose on the Paiges to meet his plane, because she didn't think, at this time of year particularly, it was a good idea for the Commodore to drive to the airport. If there was any explanation, it passed from mother to mother and never got as far as Charlotte. It wouldn't have been Oliver's explanation anyway. She was still waiting for that.

So Charlotte, her mother, and Commodore Shattuck went to collect Oliver on Thursday, through a blustery, rough, gray afternoon. Oliver appeared, suitcase in hand, and frowned when he saw them. By way of greeting, he said, "What are you doing here, Uncle Sam? Are you sure you should have come?"

The Commodore smiled fiercely at him and replied, "Of course I should! Anyway, you weren't there to stop me."

Their exchange struck Charlotte as a little odd, and she thought she detected an undercurrent of annoyance in the Commodore's joviality.

"What about Amos?" asked Oliver, changing the subject.

9

"Is he all right? Has he been good?"

The Commodore drew his tangled eyebrows together in an exaggerated scowl. "Oh, just dandy. He's spent the whole weekend looking hangdog and knocking things off tables and demanding to go out, the wretched beast. I think he's got fleas. He looks like the kind of dog who'd get fleas."

On the way home, Oliver talked politely about Washington and the weather and a concert he'd been taken to and how his mother and stepfather were. The Commodore said he needed a path shoveled through the backyard to the bird feeders. Charlotte said the skiing was good in Estabrook Woods, on the new snow. At the Commodore's house, Oliver thanked Mrs. Paige formally for sparing the time to meet him.

Mrs. Paige drove home, shaking her head. "What a peculiar boy he is."

Charlotte was just glad he was back again and there was some vacation left. That was about two and a half weeks ago. School had started after New Year's Day, and life had dropped back into routine. Christmas was packed carefully away for another eleven months. Still Oliver said nothing about what had really happened in Washington. Charlotte herself would have forgotten it, but for the fact that he seemed not quite the same as before he'd gone, though in precisely what way she couldn't decide.

"Hey," she said, as they crossed the top of Main Street and turned right on Monument, "what about me? Aren't you taking me home? I'm not walking, you know."

"In a bit. I've got to go home first."

"It would take you all of three minutes to drive to my house!" she exclaimed.

"Sometimes, Oliver Shattuck, you make me furious," she said. "Often, in fact."

He didn't answer.

Chapter Two

THEY CROSSED THE SNOWY RIVER AND HE PULLED UP IN THE Commodore's driveway. There was a light in the front room, but the rest of the house was dark. "You wait here—I'll be back in a few minutes," he said, and was out of the car and halfway to the kitchen door before she knew it.

"Oh, no." She remembered vividly the first time she had ever entered Commodore Shattuck's house, almost three years ago, when she and Oliver, hardly acquainted and deeply suspicious of each other, had, under very complicated circumstances, fallen into the Coolidges' duck pond on a raw April afternoon. She had come out bone-cold, covered in mud, and utterly miserable. It had all been Oliver's fault and he hadn't been the least bit nice about it. With the greatest unwillingness, he had taken her to his great-uncle's house—it was nearest—and left her stranded in the kitchen on an island of newspapers while he went to get clean and dry. Commodore Shattuck, on the other hand, had been unexpectedly comforting and solicitous when he found her there though he barely knew who she was. In the intervening time they had become good friends, and she felt not the slightest hesitancy about following Oliver into the house now.

The kitchen was warm and full of a tantalizing stew smell. There was an electric crock-pot simmering quietly on one of the counters. Charlotte's mouth watered involuntarily. Oliver had disappeared deeper into the house by the time she got there. She could hear the scrabbling of toenails on the bare hall floor and an excited wuffling noise, not quite a bark. Amos. For some reason Oliver had left him home that afternoon. Ordinarily Amos went along, invited or not. If you got Oliver, you got Amos. Except for school, they had become increasingly inseparable. He was about two years old, very large, and appeared still to be growing into his feet.

Charlotte headed for the voices: Oliver's quite clear, the Commodore's an indistinct mumble. Oliver met her in the living room doorway.

"I thought you were waiting in the car."

"Well, I'm not."

"How about some cocoa then?" he asked unexpectedly. "You don't really have homework."

"But—"

His mood had changed utterly, he was quite cheerful. "You can help. We'll do English muffins with cream cheese and olives."

"Oliver," she said, exasperated, to his back.

He switched on lights in the kitchen, pulled mugs out of a cupboard, put the kettle on to boil, lifted the lid of the crock-pot, peered inside, nodded, replaced it, all the while humming under his breath. It sounded like "God Rest You Merry, Gentlemen." Amos came shambling out to help, lacing himself affectionately between Oliver's legs, pausing to snuffle Charlotte's hands in greeting. She hastily lifted them out of reach and took off her parka.

She wasn't overly fond of animals, though she tolerated them; she lived quite amicably with her brother Eliot's cats, but they were independent, relatively undemanding creatures. Amos was the most peculiar dog she had ever seen. He was gray and woolly, with a long, blunt-nosed, homely head. He looked as if he'd been put together from several different-sized, do-it-yourself dog kits. He was big, but his front legs appeared to be shorter than his hind legs; he gave the impression of going downhill, whether walking, shambling, or hurtling. He had a long tail, rather sparsely covered with coarse gray hair, as if whoever had assembled him had begun to run short of covering at the hind end and had stretched what was left as far as possible.

He had been thrown out of a car at the dead end of the Schulyers' road. Dan had found him: a miserable, scrawny little animal, tied with a piece of rope to a cinderblock. That was fortunate, under the circumstances, otherwise he would probably have strayed onto Route 2 and been squashed. Dan, of course, had taken him home.

Pat, a notorious soft touch, had agreed to let the orphan stay until Dan could find him another home. "But," she said, emphatically and repeatedly, and in everyone's hearing, including Charlotte and Oliver's, "we are not adding another member to this family. He cannot stay, Daniel." It was obvious that Alice wholeheartedly agreed. Alice was the opinionated yellow dog who belonged to Pat's brother, Skip. Her maternal instincts were not in the least stirred by the wretched waif; she regarded it with grave suspicion and was even heard to growl gently when she thought it was taking liberties with her family. "That settles it," said Pat.

So Dan began to look for an adoptive family. To Charlotte, the puppy was only a mild curiosity and would have been soon forgotten if, to everyone's astonishment, Oliver had not suddenly announced that he and his Uncle Sam would take it.

"What?" said Pat doubtfully. "Are you sure? I think he's going to be—um—quite large."

"He isn't much to look at," Kath pointed out critically. "In fact—"

"Neither would you be if someone dropped you out of a car," said Dan.

"Yes. I'm sure we'll take him. We're going to call him Amos."

"Amos? Why Amos?" Kath asked.

"Why not?" countered Oliver.

So Amos went to live at the Commodore's house, where he quickly settled in and, like bread dough, doubled in bulk and kept on growing. He was a very moist dog, always licking exposed skin wherever he could find it, ingratiating, rather simple, annoyingly eager to please. Oliver had begun taking him to obedience school when he was a year old.

"Amos," said Oliver sternly, after tripping over him for

13

the second time, "go and lie *down*."

Amos shrank together and shuffled over to the back door, where he lay along the bottom crack like a large piece of weather stripping. He followed Oliver's every movement with his almond-shaped eyes. Charlotte watched Oliver too, but without Amos's adoration.

"Why wouldn't you stay at the farm?" she asked finally. "You broke up a good game."

He spread muffins without pausing. "Oh, I don't know. You should always stop before it gets to be a bore. There's tomorrow."

"Andy works after school, and Kath's got basketball."

"Open the olives, will you? All those people get to me after a while."

"They're your friends," Charlotte pointed out crisply.

"So? They still get to me. And . . ." he said with disarming honesty, ". . . I'm sure there are times when they can't stand *me*. I know there are times when you can't."

Charlotte flattened her lips. This line of conversation was getting her nowhere. Oliver was very clever at using his own faults as a defense, stating them baldly before anyone could criticize him for them. Adults were fond of saying that admitting your shortcomings was half the battle. In Oliver's case, Charlotte was unconvinced. "You didn't even give an excuse for leaving," she said.

"So?" he said again, sounding impatient. "You're nicer than I am. I wanted to leave, so I did. If you'd wanted to stay you could have, but you obviously didn't. Anyhow, with us gone they could play hockey. They were probably glad to see us leave."

But she knew they weren't. Dan, Cindy, Carl, and the Williamses maybe, but not Kath and Andy, and she suspected Oliver knew it as well as she did. The balance among them had become increasingly complex; they weren't four kids anymore, they were two boys and two girls. And added to that, Andy and Kath were brother and sister. Charlotte gazed unhappily at the olives, knowing she couldn't say any more because she didn't want to get into a discussion of it with Oliver, not now.

"Besides," said Oliver briskly, disregarding her expression, "Uncle Sam will be glad to see you. He doesn't get out much in this kind of weather and he hates being cooped up, it makes him very disagreeable."

So she was to be used as a buffer, thought Charlotte mutinously. And then—oh, well, and followed Oliver out of the kitchen.

The living room was a pocket of light and heat in the cool, shadowy house. Almost everyone Charlotte knew lived through the New England winters this way: heating only a few of the rooms in their houses and closing off all the others until warm weather. They were used to adding layers of clothing indoors as well as out. Even Charlotte's father, who passionately resented being cold in his own house, had begun to close doors and turn the thermostat down several degrees after last winter's heating bills. Although the Commodore's kitchen had felt warm when she'd first come in, once she'd taken off her parka, Charlotte had begun to feel chilly. But the living room was genuinely cozy, even hot. It was small, and there was a large electric heater glowing orange on the hearth. The air was dense and smelled strongly of wintergreen, and curtains were drawn across the windows.

Commodore Shattuck was sitting in his favorite brown bulging easy chair with pieces of the Sunday *Globe* drifted over his knees and around him on the floor. Charlotte, opening the door for Oliver, who was carrying the tray, caught a glimpse of him with his head back against a cushion, eyes closed. Then Amos bumbled in, twisting sections of paper under his great feet, and snuffled the Commodore's hands.

"Here! What are you doing, you terrible dog? Now look at the mess!" exclaimed the Commodore gruffly. "Thought you were teaching this brute manners, Oliver." He reached out and tugged one of Amos's ragged ears. Amos wriggled in ecstasy. Commodore Shattuck looked up at Charlotte. "Ah. Good. Excuse me if I don't get up. Seems to be someone standing on m'feet. Wretched beast. Skating good?"

"Um, yes," said Charlotte. "Yes, it was." She'd long since gotten over her shyness with Oliver's fierce little great-uncle; it wasn't that that made her awkward now. It was what she'd seen in that moment before he'd roused himself, just after she'd opened the door. She had seen the face of a tired old man, and it gave her a jolt. Oliver nudged her, perhaps accidentally, as he carried the tray past and set it on the table. "We played Fox and Geese with paths on the ice," she said, recovering herself. "Do you know Fox and Geese?"

"Of course I do. Haven't thought of it in years, though. Damn silly game, but fun. Used to enjoy winter when I was your age. Still would if I had the chance." He shot a look at Oliver.

"I won," said Oliver ignoring it.

"Only by default," Charlotte declared.

"I wasn't tagged, was I? I was still standing up, wasn't I?"

"I wouldn't have been caught either, if Andy hadn't run into me."

"Poor loser."

"Andy, eh? How are the Schuylers then? Andy and Kath, and that young one—Daniel? Daniel. Haven't seen them since—" He broke off, frowning.

"They're fine," said Oliver. "Here, Uncle Sam, and here's a napkin for underneath."

"In case I spill, you mean."

Oliver said sharply, "Don't be silly."

"Well, I did, you know," said the Commodore to Charlotte. "A whole bowl of soup last week. Rug-colored soup—minestrone." He grinned. "Bet you can't tell."

Charlotte looked around at the floor and grinned back. "Nope."

"That thing"—he nodded at Amos—"thought he'd died and gone to heaven. Noodles and chunks of meat everywhere. 'Bout all you can say for him, he's good at cleaning up that kind of mess." Amos thumped his tail in agreement. " 'Course *Oliver* won't let me forget it. Never knew a boy to fuss so."

"Oh, Uncle Sam," said Oliver in exasperation. "Look, I gave Charlotte a napkin, too."

"I *never* spill," said Charlotte virtuously.

"Mmmph," snorted the Commodore. "Nice to be perfect. He wasn't going to bring you in, you know, this nephew of mine."

16

"I'm used to that."

Oliver drew his eyebrows together; he didn't like being needled. "Uncle Sam, did you remember your pill?"

"Charlotte, will you listen to him? This is what it's come to—what I have to live with," grumbled the Commodore. "He's convinced I'm a feeble old man."

"I only asked if you'd taken your pill. I'll bet you haven't."

"Oh no, I'm such a poor forgetful ruin of the man I once was," replied his great-uncle in a thin, quavery voice. "Can't keep anything in my numb old brain for two minutes together. Oh, I'm lucky to have you looking after me."

"Uncle Sam," said Oliver warningly. He got up and went to the mantelpiece. On it stood a brown bottle with a prescription label.

"One pill more or less, what does it matter."

Charlotte looked doubtfully at the Commodore as he said it, and to her relief he grinned wickedly and gave her a wink. They were playing games with each other as usual, the Commodore and Oliver. She was seldom taken in by it anymore, but this afternoon something felt slightly different—or was it her mood?

"Sometimes, Uncle Sam, I wonder why I bother," said Oliver. He put the bottle down with a little thump.

"So do I, my boy, so do I. If I were you, I wouldn't. I'd go right away and leave me to decay all by myself and serve me right, too."

"Your cocoa's getting cold," said Charlotte to neither of them in particular. "Do you know what I think? I think you deserve each other. No one else would put up with either one of you."

"There," said the Commodore. "What have I told you? She's clever, this one. She's onto our secret."

Instead of coming back with a sharp rejoinder, Oliver stared into his mug and only said, "Hmmm."

They settled into the lazy warmth of the room and the Commodore told stories about skating when he was young, growing up in the town. He had a tremendous store of anecdotes, many of which bordered on the slanderous as Mr. Paige observed when Charlotte passed them on to her fam-

ily. Years ago there were enormous skating parties and bon-
fires, and ladies skated in long skirts holding onto chairs for
balance. When the river froze, they would skate for miles
along it, north to Billerica, or south toward Sudbury. They
carried flasks and drank hot toddies and spiced cider, and
Viola Wardlaw used to make wonderful cinnamon dough-
nuts. One winter Frank Bullard, Andy and Kath's grandfather, went through the ice under the railroad bridge by the
boathouse. When they hauled him out, his hair and mous-
tache froze, but they filled him with brandy and he had to
be carried home. He was none the worse for his dunking,
except his mother, who was a strict teetotaler, almost didn't
forgive him for not drowning.

"Did anyone ever drown?" asked Charlotte. She had
skated on the river herself and found it exciting, but never
quite trusted it entirely. Underneath, the water still moved,
dark and bitter, pushing and dragging and causing the ice to
twang and snap. There were springs hidden in the stiff gray
bushes, where the ice was weak, and under bridges lay strips
of black, open water to remind you of what a thin, imper-
manent skin it was you were skating on.

"Not skating. No one I knew anyway. Saw a dog once,
though. During a thaw—the ice was rotten. He got out too
far tracking something—fox probably—and it crumbled. Every
time he got his paws on the edge it crumbled further, and no
one could get out to him. The cold and the current carried
him off and they never found him."

"How awful!" Charlotte shivered.

"Not so bad," said the Commodore musingly. "Hypo-
thermia, they call it—freezing to death. Not supposed to be
painful, just slipping off to sleep."

"But trapped under the ice," she protested. "Not able to
get through it to the air."

"Fast," said the Commodore. "You'd hardly know."

"What a morbid conversation," broke in Oliver. "Do you
know what time it is?"

Charlotte glanced at her watch. "Holy cow! Six-thirty.
I didn't notice. I've got to get home." She'd been enjoying
herself and lost track, and she felt guilty when she thought

of Andy and Kath. She hadn't intended to spend the rest of the afternoon at the Commodore's house. She hadn't intended to set foot in it.

"I suppose you want me to drive you," said Oliver ungraciously.

"I'm not walking."

"Oliver, sometimes I despair of you, my boy." The Commodore knitted his tangled eyebrows in disapproval.

"It wouldn't hurt her. No, don't say it—I'll get my jacket." He picked up the tray and went out.

"Don't you let him get away with that kind of thing," said Commodore Shattuck sternly. "It isn't good for him. I mean it, you know."

Charlotte smiled at him and impulsively put out her hand. He took it and gave it a squeeze. "I won't," she said.

In the chilly kitchen Oliver was rinsing out the cocoa mugs. "Where's yours?"

"Sorry, I left it." She went back. Commodore Shattuck had relaxed in his chair and shrunk down a little so that he looked smaller. He seemed to have gone to sleep, his jaws slack, his eyes shut. The shapeless unease she'd felt on first seeing him returned, and she paused, uncertain, but Oliver came in behind her with Amos at his heels, and the Commodore's eyelids fluttered up. "Uncle Sam, I'm going to take Charlotte now, all right? We'll have supper when I get back. I'll only be a few minutes."

"All right, all right. There's no hurry, I'm not going anywhere." He sounded faintly irritable. "I suppose you're going to leave that creature."

Amos looked longingly up at Oliver, who was zipping his jacket, and Oliver said, "Yes. Amos, you stay."

As they drove back toward Charlotte's house, she asked reluctantly—because asking gave substance to the formless concern—"He's all right, isn't he? Your great-uncle?"

Without looking from the road ahead, Oliver said, "Why wouldn't he be? What makes you ask?"

She gave her head a shake. "Just that he seemed a little—well, tired, I guess."

"Aren't you ever tired?"

19

"Of course, but—"

"It's the cold weather. He feels it more than he used to, and I told you, he can't get out. He has arthritis, you know. Lots of people have arthritis. George Schuyler has arthritis. Mrs. Morse has—"

"You made your point," said Charlotte. "I was only asking a friendly question."

"And I've answered, okay?" As he turned the car right, down Main Street, he asked, "Do you know how old Uncle Sam is?"

"No. Not exactly. I hadn't thought about it." He'd been old ever since she'd known him, his hair white, his face netted with wrinkles, but she didn't consciously think of him as an old man. He was such a vigorous person: full of plans for the afternoon, tomorrow, next week—not just joining in things, but instigating them.

"He's eighty-two. He doesn't seem that old, does he?" Oliver's tone was challenging.

"No," she agreed. Eighty-two sounded very old.

"I guess when you're eighty-two you're entitled to spend a quiet Sunday afternoon at home reading the paper without having everyone think you aren't well."

"Oh, for heaven's sake!" Charlotte welcomed the chance to shift from concern for the Commodore to annoyance at Oliver. "I only asked—"

"Okay, I know."

Chapter Three

"DIDN'T OLIVER COME IN WITH YOU?" ASKED MRS. PAIGE FROM
the kitchen doorway as Charlotte unlaced her boots. "I saw
the car in the driveway and I thought—"

"No," said Charlotte. "I didn't invite him." She didn't
explain that there would have been no point, he would only
have turned her down. His mind was plainly fixed on going
home.

"Oh? Nothing wrong, is there?" Opening the refrigerator,
her mother frowned a little as she began to examine little
packages and covered dishes. She pulled them out, then put
them back again, searching for something. "I do wish your
sister would stop bringing me bean curd. I know it's healthy
and infinitely versatile, but I get so tired of hunting up ways
to disguise it."

"You could just throw it out," suggested Charlotte, who
actively disliked the stuff. Where was the virtue in food that
had no taste, even if it was good for you? Taste, to Charlotte,
was one of the main reasons for eating.

Mrs. Paige sighed. "I can't quite bring myself to do that,
at least not until it's turned green and furry. It isn't all that
cheap."

"That's Deb's problem. You don't *ask* her to bring it. Besides, she gets it wholesale."

"I suppose that's much the best way to look at it, darling.
There—mushroom quiche. I knew it was here somewhere.
Will that do for supper?" She held out a half-filled pie pan

21

and Charlotte nodded. "Have you and Oliver had a fight?"

"No. I don't think so, though I don't always know we have until afterward," she said wryly. "He's just being antisocial, that's all. He wouldn't stay at the Schuylers' either."

"I've hardly laid eyes on him since we picked him up at the airport. Or Sam Shattuck, for that matter. Is everything all right there?"

"Why shouldn't it be?" said Charlotte, not looking at her mother. She didn't want to worry about Oliver and the Commodore, she wanted to be told it wasn't necessary.

Mrs. Paige cut the quiche into pieces that would fit into the toaster-oven and set the temperature. "No reason, darling, I just wondered."

"We went to the Commodore's after skating this afternoon and had cocoa—that's why I'm late. He was telling stories about skating on the river years ago—you know his stories. You forget you should be doing other things."

Her mother smiled and nodded. "You can either set the table or make the salad. It's just the two of us, so we might as well eat in here where it's cosier. We never gave a thought to the cost of heating this house when we bought it twenty-four years ago. Nobody worried about that kind of thing. Now it's one of the first questions I ask—how much are the fuel bills."

"But anyone thinking of buying this house will ask the same thing, won't they?" Charlotte elected to set the table; she hated washing greens.

"Not people with pots of money. 'Lovely Victorian house on half-acre of choice land, river frontage, three and a half bathrooms, walk to town center.' Marge Simms doesn't think we'll have any trouble finding a buyer for it."

"It isn't as if we're *poor*," objected Charlotte. "We aren't, are we? We don't *have* to move."

"It depends on your point of view. No, we aren't poor, but we don't need this house anymore, darling. It's enormous for three people. The taxes and upkeep are very expensive—we're paying for space we can't begin to use, and there's no point. It isn't a very convenient house to keep clean, either.

I'm tired of it. It makes sense to move now, before your father retires, and get settled."

"Where is he tonight?"

"At a meeting in Cambridge. I can't keep track of them all. He seems to spend as much time in town now as he ever did when he worked there." Mrs. Paige gave her head a shake. "I wish he'd find something to do with himself out here—gardening or golf, something he can keep on with once he leaves the museum."

They sat across from each other, sharing the warm, bright room, leftover quiche, and a spinach salad. Mrs. Paige poured them each a glass of white wine from a carafe and drank hers down while Charlotte sipped. It was nice to be just the two of them, unhurried and companionable. Charlotte liked having her mother all to herself.

After a while she said, "I can't really imagine Daddy retired. It doesn't seem possible somehow."

"I know. To be honest, I have trouble imagining it, too. And I'm afraid he isn't thinking about it at all. Still, there's no point in worrying, it isn't for a couple of years yet," she said, deliberately cheerful. "And right now I think we all need a change. I certainly do. Twenty-four years in one house is long enough."

"*I* haven't lived here twenty-four years," Charlotte pointed out. "You haven't found anything else yet, have you?"

Her mother shook her head. "I've got several appointments next week. There's one on Strawberry Hill Road and another out near Middlesex School. I'm still not sure we shouldn't consider Carlisle. You're in high school, so it wouldn't mean you'd have to change schools."

"Just so long as we live more than a mile from it this time. I hate having to walk in the winter."

"The part I dread is having people come and look at this house. We'll have to keep it unnaturally tidy all the time."

"Not my room, we won't. They'll just have to imagine what it looks like," declared Charlotte. She helped herself to another small slice of quiche. The two remaining cats, Lapsang Souchong and Hu Kwah, drowsed in front of the heat

23

vent under the sink, heads back, paws folded inward. Beyond the kitchen the rest of the house was dark and empty. Charlotte's two brothers and sister, all much older than she, the two other cats and the pair of rabbits—thank heaven!— were gone. Max, the eldest, had been away at college when Charlotte was born; now he had a wife and a two-year-old daughter and lived in Cambridge. Deb and Eliot had been at home until a couple of years ago. Then Eliot had gone off to study wildlife management in Montana, to everyone's surprise, especially hers. Less than twelve months later, Deb gave up teaching art in a private elementary school and sank all her money and what she could borrow in a natural foods store. She rented a little building in the middle of Concord— a shop with an apartment over it—took one of the cats, and went into business for herself. Max and Jean had adopted placid old Camomile when they bought their own house. So now there were only Charlotte, her parents, and two cats, living in the house where Charlotte had lived all her life.

It has always seemed to her a comfortable size, with enough room for six people to be private when they wanted to be; but with the departure of Eliot and Deb, it had grown suddenly huge and unnaturally quiet. Although she had adjusted, the emptiness still caught her off-guard once in a while, and she experienced moments of acute longing—for the time when everything in her life had seemed permanent. The house was a link with that time; it was also a painful reminder of all that had changed. The thought of leaving it made her sad, but not as sad as she felt it should.

"It's strange to think of other people actually living here," she said slowly, after a silence. "I don't like it much."

"It'll be different," said Mrs. Paige briskly, "when we've found the right house to move into. You'll stop looking back and start looking forward. It'll be fun, fixing up something new."

"You do it all the time in your job."

"Yes, but that's for other people, and I have to do what they want, even when I know they're wrong, which they often are." She poured herself another glass of wine. "Other people's taste is seldom as good as mine," she said wryly.

24

"I've heard you getting your own way with clients," said Charlotte.

"I have my reputation as an interior designer to protect," replied her mother. "I can't let them make dreadful mistakes—it would reflect on me. Not to change the subject, but do you know what I've got in the freezer? A Sara Lee pound cake and a pint of double chocolate ice cream."

Charlotte's eyes lit. Reluctantly, she confessed, "I had cocoa and muffins at Oliver's—"

"But think of all the calories you burned skating."

She brightened. "Do you really think so? If you promise not to tell Deb—"

"Of course not. It's none of her business. And don't you tell her that I let her bean curd get moldy."

"It's a deal." They grinned at each other conspiratorially and with deep mutual satisfaction settled to dishes of pound cake a la mode.

"I don't care what your sister claims," declared Mrs. Paige, "frozen yogurt is *not* the same."

"And carob doesn't taste a bit like chocolate," added Charlotte. "But Deb doesn't really care. Food isn't very important to her."

"That's why she stays thin, my pet. It isn't virtue, it's natural inclination, so she can't take credit for it the way you and I can."

"Some people," said Charlotte wistfully, "can eat whatever they want and not gain weight. Kath's like that."

"Kath gets lots of exercise. Did you all go to Sam's for cocoa this afternoon?"

Charlotte concentrated on taking very small bites and making them last. "No, just Oliver and I."

Mrs. Paige's expression grew thoughtful. "Darling, has Oliver ever talked to you about why he came back from Washington so early?"

"No, and I haven't asked him. Because of his mother, I suppose. You never told me what she said when she called after Christmas. She talked to you long enough."

"She didn't go into detail, she just said it seemed pointless to make him stay when he made it so obvious he didn't want to be there. It was a difficult situation, I gather."

"It didn't have to be. She knew he didn't want to go in the first place," said Charlotte. "I don't see why she made him. Oliver and Commodore Shattuck get along perfectly well together. Oliver's been here longer than he's been anywhere else since his parents got divorced. Why doesn't she leave him alone? His father does."

Mrs. Paige took a long breath. "It isn't quite that simple, Charlotte. Regardless of what you think about her, Paula's his mother and she's still responsible for him. Though you may not believe it, she does love him. You're Oliver's friend, don't forget, so you hear his side of things."

"And you hear hers," countered Charlotte.

Mrs. Paige considered her empty wine glass for a minute. "Well, don't let's argue about it—I'm sure there are things neither of us knows. What about having them to dinner one night next week—Sam and Oliver? It seems like a long time since they've been here, and I've been feeling guilty about it. But what with Christmas and having the baby here while Max and Jean went to New York—"

"It was only three days," said Charlotte, grinning.

"The longest three days I can ever remember. I still haven't found all the things we had to put out of reach."

"But you found the Zweiback under the dining room rug."

"I hope that's the only place she hid it. What do you think?"

"I looked in the living room."

"No, about having Sam and Oliver to dinner."

"Sure. Why not?" Charlotte looked hard at her mother. "Mom, you aren't worried about them for some reason, are you?"

"Not really, no. But I did promise Paula to keep an eye on things, darling, and I feel some responsibility. Besides, I enjoy them and so does your father."

"Everything's fine," said Charlotte firmly. "I'd tell you if I thought it wasn't."

"I know, of course you would."

Chapter Four

DURING THE NIGHT THE WIND CHANGED. BY MORNING THE temperature hovered around freezing, and the sky was clogged with sullen gray cloud. It was a raw, cheerless day. In civics class, her last before lunch, Charlotte looked out the window to see large flakes of snow blur the dark fringe of trees on the white hill above the school. She glanced across the classroom to see if Andy Schuyler had noticed, but she could tell from the benign expression on his face that he was deep in daydreams about summer. He certainly wasn't concentrating on the American judicial system as he should have been. Doubtless he was laying out rows of beans and peas, estimating hills of squash and quantities of cauliflower, cabbage and beets. For a split second, she grasped the thread of his thoughts and felt, piercingly, the hot crumbly brown earth between her fingers, smelled the spicy fragrance of warm tomato plants, saw corn tassels against the blue blazing August sky. It was pure sensation and gone in an instant, replaced by Mrs. Inch's crisp voice explaining about Constitutional law and the Supreme Court. Resolutely, Charlotte set her mind to the subject, which she didn't find uninteresting.

When the class was over, Charlotte, Beth Quinn, and Tony Costello carried the discussion with them through the halls, toward the cafeteria, unmindful of Andy, who attached himself to them but didn't say anything.

"I don't see why a bunch of judges in black robes sitting

27

in a mausoleum in Washington should be able to tell me how to run my life," declared Beth.

"All they do," said Tony with exaggerated patience, "is interpret the Constitution. They don't just arbitrarily decide how they want things to be, you know."

"But they're fallible," Beth pointed out, "just like anyone else."

"They're bound to make mistakes sometimes, and they must all have biases," Charlotte agreed. "I don't see how anybody can be absolutely neutral."

"That's why there are nine—they balance each other," said Tony.

"What about when one person's civil rights conflict with someone else's? Or letting someone else decide what isn't good for you so you can't have it? Are you going to let someone do that?" Beth demanded.

Tony shrugged. "So what's new? My parents do it all the time."

"Suppose it really is harmful, though," said Charlotte. "Like pornography?"

"Now you're talking."

Beth ignored him. "Can't you make up your own mind about it? How can you be sure it really is trash if you never see it yourself? Do you just accept another person's opinion?"

"One person's trash is another person's art," said Tony wisely. "You ever been to the Combat Zone, Andy?"

"What? No," said Andy.

"Have you?" Beth sounded curious.

"Sure. It's not so much really. Bookstores, clubs with pictures out front, dirty movies." He grinned suggestively. "I'll take you there sometime if you want."

"Thanks," said Beth dryly. "Sounds like a teriffic date."

They drifted away from Charlotte and Andy in the cafeteria, no longer talking about the Supreme Court, but about movies. Charlotte went through the line, while Andy, who brought his lunch, picked a table for them. Monday was the only day they shared lunch period and they always sat together. It was a habit. Every now and then Charlotte felt the merest twinge of rebellion, not so much against Andy as against having it taken for granted, at having no choice. But she'd come out of the line with her tray, and there he'd be, waiting for her, and she couldn't hurt his feelings by sitting anywhere else. They'd been friends since eighth grade.

Besides, she enjoyed his company. If she was willing to work at it, it was possible to get him to talk about something other than the farm, which was his single greatest passion. She discovered, sometime into their friendship, that he liked reading and had actually read quite a lot of books, though he did it almost entirely in the winter, when the farm was dormant. His tastes in literature were definite and fairly narrow, and he didn't bother with anything that failed to interest him in the first page or two. "But you can't always tell about a book in two pages," Charlotte would argue. "Lots of books start slowly, you have to work into them."

"I don't read fast enough," he'd reply, apologetic, but inflexible. "There isn't enough time. If I don't like the beginning, I figure it's better to find something else. There're always lots more."

When Charlotte recommended a book to him, he would make a special effort with it, however, and when he liked it he'd tell her so. When he didn't, he simply wouldn't mention it unless she badgered him, as if he were afraid she'd be annoyed. Over and over she told him that she *liked* a good argument. When she could drag them out of him, he frequently had interesting opinions. But he preferred to avoid controversy, and he liked to think things over before he spoke. That was why he seldom volunteered in class, not because he was dull or hadn't done any of the work, as she had once thought.

"Too bad you couldn't stay longer yesterday," he said as she sat down and handed him his milk. He paid her and she always bought it for him. "This snow's so wet it'll ruin the ice until it freezes again."

"I know." She didn't look at him. "We had to get home."

"It wasn't that late."

He didn't usually push. She felt guilty and it made her irritable. "I told you, I had homework." She bit into her hamburger and chewed in silence. It was overdone and tough—they always were. It was better to eat without thinking about

29

them. To change the subject, she said, "Maybe you won't have to work this afternoon if it keeps snowing."

He gave his head a rueful shake. "No luck. They never close supermarkets. And if we're going to have a storm there'll be twice as many people buying things in case they can't get out tomorrow. You can sit at home nice and warm and think of me slogging around the parking lot in the slush collecting wet carts." Then his face brightened. "I've got Saturday off, though. Maybe we could do something—go tobogganing or skiing—if the snow's any good. Or the pond might be okay by then."

"All of us?" asked Charlotte.

"Sure. Maybe Commodore Shattuck would even come. He hasn't done anything with us this winter, not like last year. I miss having him along, you know?" He looked across at Charlotte questioningly. "He's all right, isn't he?"

"Of course he's all right! Why wouldn't he be? Why does everyone think there's something wrong with him?" she exclaimed angrily.

Andy looked startled. "I don't know. Does everyone? I— it's just that I haven't seen him in a while. I thought he might have a cold or 'flu or something."

"When would you see him? You're always working."

"Yeah, I know." He made a face. "But I've got to get the money for a new carburetor this winter. We have to have the tractor by spring, we've *got* to. This is the only way I can do it. It's going to be awfully tight anyway. Still," he added with determination, "it'll work out, it's bound to."

Charlotte was sorry for her outburst. Andy had only asked out of interest and concern, and there *was* nothing wrong— she had no reason to snap at him. "Oliver says his arthritis gets worse in cold weather."

Andy nodded sagely. "Like my granddad. Got so he couldn't get out of bed in the winter. He'd lie upstairs and thump with his stick when he wanted something. And then you'd run up and he'd've forgotten what it was. Half the time I think he just wanted company. Gramma said not to bother, he thumped because he was bored, but someone always had to go in case he really did need something." He

30

opened an aluminum package of Fig Newtons. "Have one?"

"Thanks. Did he ever? Need help, I mean?"

"Oh, yes. Only he didn't thump, not with his stick. He fell out of bed and it sounded the same. And he wasn't hurt, so it was all right. Saturday's okay then?"

She nodded. "It is with me. I'll tell Oliver. I'm sure we could borrow the Commodore's toboggan, even if he doesn't come, and maybe we could all go there afterward."

"Skip's had this idea for next summer—see what you think. He says we ought to grow herbs, a lot of them. People are into that kind of thing these days. He thinks we could market them through your sister's store—it'd be the perfect place. Tarragon, basil, dill, that sort of stuff. He thinks we could get pretty fancy prices."

"You aren't, by any chance, talking about the farm, are you?" asked Charlotte.

Her sarcasm was lost on him. "Of course I mean the farm. What do you think? Would she go for the idea?"

Charlotte gave up. "Probably. Do you want me to ask her?"

"Skip said he would. But maybe it wouldn't hurt if you said something, too. Sometimes I think winter'll never end," he said with a sigh, screwing up the aluminum foil into a tight little ball. He winged it at the nearest trash barrel and it went in neatly.

"Cheer up," said Charlotte, "it always does."

It was still snowing by the end of school: wet, heavy flakes, mixed with freezing rain, thoroughly unpleasant. All exposed pavements were glazed with a shell of ice. Just before the last bell a voice on the PA system cancelled after-school activities: no basketball practice for Kath, no chorus for Charlotte. And Oliver got away from school before Charlotte had a chance to talk to him about Saturday. He could be annoyingly elusive. With resignation she faced the walk home, wrapping her books in a plastic bag and pulling her hat down to her eyebrows.

Away from the noise and congestion of the emptying high school, Charlotte entered an anonymous, muffled landscape, treacherous underfoot, invisible beyond a few feet. She made her way carefully down the long exposed hill, with buses trundling slowly past in the gloom. Cars crept along Thoreau Street, thrusting into the snow with their headlights. She hugged her books against her chest, put her head down and withdrew as far as she could into herself. When she reached the traffic lights at Sudbury Road, she pushed the pedestrian button and waited. When she saw WALK appear in green letters, dim through the shifting snow, she stepped into the road. Ahead of her, a car approached the intersection, slowed to stop and kept right on coming, straight for her, skewed sideways across the slick road, coming and coming, in a kind of heart-cramping slow motion. Charlotte, seeing it slide toward her, froze like a rabbit, unbelieving. It skidded to rest against the curb, less than two feet from where she stood, close enough to touch. Through the crusted windshield she saw the pale, stiff face of the driver, eyes wide and blank, mouth half-open. They stared at each other in shock for an endless moment—Charlotte couldn't tell if it was a man or a woman behind the wheel—then she gathered her scattered wits and resumed her separate journey, leaving the car behind. She was unharmed; there seeemd no point in exchanging words, even if she could think of any.

Chapter Five

ON THE FAR CURB, CHARLOTTE HESITATED. SHE FELT HOT inside her clothing, her skin prickled; going home to an empty house seemed suddenly unbearable. She needed to make contact with another person, and both her parents were at work.

So was Deb, but Deb was accessible. She was weighing out bags of red lentils when Charlotte got to the Magic Cupboard and singing along with Neil Diamond on the radio. Singing *against* better described Deb's efforts, actually; she had none of Eliot's musical ability. The store was empty except for Earl Grey, stalking moodily around the counters, his tail twitching.

"Filthy day," observed Deb, leaving Neil to get on with "Brother Love's Traveling Salvation Show" by himself. "For one shining moment I thought you were a paying customer instead of a relative. I've had three since I opened."

"I'm not surprised," said Charlotte. "It's all ice out there. It's awful."

"Don't drip on the merchandise, will you. Why don't you hang your stuff in the back room and plug the kettle in."

"Anyway," Charlotte said as she reappeared, "some of your paying customers *are* relatives."

"Here, you can be useful—you can fasten the bags shut."

"So is some of your unpaid help. I saw someone skid right across the road on my way here."

"People have no sense at all," declared Deb. "Shouldn't drive in weather like this. Everything ought to be shut."

"You aren't."

"No, but I live over the shop—I don't have to go anywhere, and as long as I'm here, I might as well keep the door unlocked for the idiots who *do* come out. Their money's as good as anyone else's."

"I hope I don't qualify as an idiot," said Charlotte. She was feeling much better, her balance restored by Deb's brusqueness.

"There's a new herb tea I want to try."

"What is it? The last one tasted like old grass clippings."

"This one's exotic. Chinese Almond Blossom. The salesman says it's delicious."

"He would. He's pushing it," Charlotte pointed out.

"Cynic," replied Deb tolerantly. "Smells good. Here."

Charlotte wrapped her cold fingers around the hot mug and sniffed the steam suspiciously. "It's like drinking macaroons," she said after a couple of careful sips.

"Well, then you should like it."

"I'm not at all sure. I'd rather chew them, I think. Can I have some honey in mine?" She knew better than to ask for sugar.

"Philistine. There's a jar next to the kettle."

Charlotte stirred a couple of spoonfuls into her mug, then returned to twist fasteners onto plastic bags. They worked together comfortably, without talking. Although Charlotte wasn't altogether convinced by a lot of the merchandise Deb sold, she liked the store. It smelled of coffee beans and peanuts—Deb had machines for grinding both—dried herbs, and other unidentifiable things. It was small and full, but not cramped; it had windows and a wood floor that creaked. It occupied the first floor of a little two-story frame house tucked in back of the other stores on Main Street. To reach it, you had to go through the big parking lot behind Woolworth's.

Deb loved it. After two years she was making a modest profit and attracting an odd and likeable mixture of regular customers. In Charlotte's opinion Deb was infinitely easier to get along with than she had ever been: more relaxed and less astringent, still sharp, but less inclined to cut. In fact,

Charlotte, who had once been wary of her older sister, now found that there were things she could talk to Deb about that she had trouble sharing with anyone else. The gap between them stayed the same in years, but its significance seemed steadily to shrink.

Deb's fourth customer, a tall, round-shouldered man with a furry hat crammed around his ears, came in and after wandering about, bought half a gallon of olive oil, a small sack of lecithin, and two pounds of brown rice. When he'd gone, Deb said, "How's Mother's project coming?"

"All right, I guess. She's had trouble with the carpeting—they ran out of the dye lot in the middle of the front hall and didn't tell her. They said they didn't think it showed, but of course she saw it right away and made them take it all up again, so they're behind."

"As usual," said Deb. "But I didn't mean the condominiums, I meant the house hunting. It's still on, isn't it?"

Charlotte made a face and nodded. "She was talking last night about getting ours on the market. She hasn't found anything yet, but she's got some to look at this week. I can't help wishing we didn't have to do it until I finish high school."

"That's two and a half years," said Deb briskly. "That house is an awful waste for the three of you. Besides, you need a change to keep you from going stale."

"That's what Mom says. If you ask me, what *I* need is stability. Adolescence is a very difficult period."

Deb gave her a rueful grin. "I seem to remember that. But cheer up, you'll survive it. Then you'll find out your troubles are only beginning!"

"You're not very encouraging."

Deb's grin broadened. "Oh well, it has its brighter moments, too, and the alternative's lousy." They shifted from lentils to packing bran in two-pound bags; it was light and dusty and harder to control. "How's your social life these days?"

Charlotte sighed which spread the bran further. "That's what I mean about stability at home. Everything else is shifting around and I don't have a very good grasp on it."

"Oh?" said Deb with casual interest.

"It's the four of us—Andy and Kath and Oliver and me."

"You haven't had a falling out, have you? You're still friends?"

We're still friends, but not in the same way—at least *I* don't think it is. It's changing."

"Frankly," Deb said, "I'd be surprised if it didn't. After all, *you're* changing. I know it sounds simplistic, but you're all growing up. Relationships change because people change—or they become obsolete and die. I know from bitter personal experience. But I guess that's the only way you ever do know," she added reflectively.

"I don't know what to do about it, though," said Charlotte a little desperately.

"Do you have to do anything? Can't you just let it happen?"

"I don't know that, either."

Deb stopped measuring bran. "Ah," she said.

Charlotte drew a face on the counter in the scattered flakes, wondering why on earth she'd gotten herself into this, and how she would get herself out again. She felt Deb watching her.

"You know," said her sister after a few oppressive minutes, "you know, you've really been very lucky. Not a whole lot of kids your age have had the kind of friendship you guys have had. Four of you, doing things together, two boys and two girls. You may not believe this, but I've even envied you a bit."

Charlotte looked at her in surprise.

"Oh, I had lots of friends when I was in school, more than you have, but they were either girls or boyfriends. That's not the same. My advice, which you probably think isn't worth a damn," said Deb cheerfully, "is, as dear Nicholas would say—God bless him—not to get your knickers in a twist over what can't be helped. Be grateful for what you've had."

In spite of herself, Charlotte couldn't help a little snort of laughter. "He wouldn't really say that, would he? He always seemed too proper," she protested.

"I should know. I spent two weeks with him in London that summer."

36

"You never told us that. I thought you must have gone to see him, though."

"Of course I didn't tell you—it was *my* business. It was very educational," she continued musingly. "His mother didn't like me a bit, but I liked her even less, so it didn't matter. It would never have worked. Even Nicholas could see that."

Nicholas Boutwell-Scott was a very persistant Englishman, who, while visiting Concord several years ago, had taken a great liking to Deb. He had annoyed her no end by following her around town, attempting to strike up a conversation; her irritability seemed only to encourage him. Charlotte had had occasion to meet Nicholas several times and had privately considered him extremely attractive: handsome and dashing and humorous, if a bit overconfident. She had found Deb's hostility toward him hard to understand. But it was obvious from what she had just said that Deb hadn't been as immune to his charms as she had, at the time, pretended.

"Of course," she said judiciously, "I was far less mature at that point in my life. We had fun, but it wasn't a permanent relationship."

Charlotte turned serious. "How did you *know?*" she asked.

Deb raised her dark eyebrows. "I didn't. Not until afterward."

"But wasn't that painful?"

"Yes, I suppose it was. Look, Charlotte, most things to do with other people are painful at one time or another. They are also the source of a good deal of joy. It's a trade-off. If you close out one, you lose the other as well. This is a pretty heavy conversation, you know. I wonder if it was the tea?"

"I doubt it," said Charlotte. "I haven't drunk mine. Sorry."

"Then what's happening to make you begin pondering these bottomless questions? Anything specific?"

"Well—" she said reluctantly, "I guess it was the dance last month. I wish now we hadn't gone."

"Didn't you enjoy it?"

"I did, sort of. I mean, yes. But—"

The phone rang in the back room. Deb gave her a searching look and went to answer it. Charlotte breathed a sigh of relief. If Deb had stayed, she would have tried to straighten everything out, to make sense of it. Part of Charlotte wanted to do that very badly. But another part of her kept hoping that if she didn't, she could put the whole business away, in the back of her mind, like empty luggage in the attic, and forget about it. She could hear Deb talking, then silence, then a groan that sounded like sympathy, then more talk.

At some level, Charlotte knew that if it hadn't been the dance, it would have been something else—maybe something gentler, more gradual, though. This had been unexpectedly jarring. Every year the sophomores sponsored a Christmas dance in the high school cafeteria—for lack of big money—just before vacation. Charlotte gave it little more than a passing thought, but somehow Oliver got himself involved with the committee planning it, he never did explain how. Then it seemed to be understood that they'd all be going.

She expected Andy and Kath to refuse, Kath certainly. Kath resisted anything that meant putting on a dress. And Andy was bound to consider it a waste of time and money. Charlotte was so sure they wouldn't agree, she felt quite disappointed. It was something of a shock, therefore, when after a little hesitation they decided they'd go. There was some trouble about clothes, but nothing they thought they couldn't work out—the dance wasn't exactly formal.

The thing was, that although the four of them went together as usual, it wasn't as a group, it was as two couples: Andy with Charlotte, and Kath with Oliver. They had to work it out that way because of Andy and Kath being brother and sister. They went in the same car, sat together, swapped dances back and forth, but they were still couples, and this time—to Charlotte anyway—it made a difference. She couldn't forget it and have a good time, though the others seemed able to.

Even Kath, who was the last person she could have imagined enjoying a dance—Kath who spent her free time at sports practices or down at Alan Watts's stables cleaning up after horses, Kath who never wore skirts to school, who was customarily awkward and silent on social occasions—even Kath had a good time. There she was in a green corduroy jumper, probably her mother's, and a fresh white frilly blouse, her wild red hair swept back at the sides and tied with a piece of ribbon—quite unlike the Kath Charlotte was used to—smiling till you'd think her face would ache, willing to dance, almost talkative. And Andy was equally unfamiliar in one of his Uncle Skip's dark suits, which had obviously not been made for him. Charlotte had never seen him in a suit before; it made him seem very large and awkward. He danced the way he skated, with determination and speed rather than grace, and his hands were damp. She didn't see how he could possibly be having fun, but he assured her he was.

And Oliver. Well Oliver had grown taller during his years in Concord and lost the pinched, yellow look he had come with. He was still angular, but in a surprisingly attractive way. His suit *had* been bought for him; it fitted and made him look older. There were freshmen and sophomores, Charlotte knew, who thought Oliver was enigmatic and fascinating. Of course, they didn't know him well enough to realize that he could also be very irritating when he chose, and stubborn and imperious. She felt superior because she did know.

There was no question, she liked dancing with him. She didn't *dis*like dancing with Andy, either. But whenever she was, she couldn't help being aware of Oliver and Kath together; it pinched like a slightly tight pair of shoes. She'd look at Andy and he'd be smiling at her, inviting her to smile back, and she would. So the evening went, creating disturbance and confusion; she was sorry she'd gone, but she wouldn't *not* have gone; afraid of what was happening and excited by it.

Deb gave a short laugh, and a moment later came back. "Charlotte, that was Dad. He's in a fearful mood—he's been calling and calling the house and getting no answer. The second-floor gallery at the museum is leaking, and they've got someone lined up to come, but he can't leave until they've got it under control, so he doesn't know what time he'll be home."

"I suppose I ought to go." Charlotte looked out a window. "It's still snowing. Ugh."

"You can stay and have supper with me, if you want," offered Deb. "Skip's coming when he's through at the bank."

But Charlotte shook her head. "I'd better go and keep Mom company." She turned to her sister curiously. "Does Skip really eat the same kind of stuff you do? I somehow can't see him sitting down to a meal of soyburgers and beansprouts."

Deb gave an amused, exasperated little snort. "Shows how much you know. Anyway, that isn't all I eat. We're having chicken tonight, for your information. Stir-fried."

"You fake!" exclaimed Charlotte with a grin. "I might have known Skip could take care of himself. Yuck. Everything's soggy." She pulled on her hat and mittens.

"I'd drive you, but you're safer walking in this," said Deb. "And I can't afford to damage the van. Does Mother need anything?"

Charlotte almost said, "A pound of tofu," then thought better of it. "I don't think so. Thanks—see you."

On the way home, instead of brooding about the dance, Charlotte speculated instead on the interesting relationship that seemed to be developing between her sister and the Schuylers' uncle, Skip Bullard. Skip was Eliot's contemporary and best friend. At one time Charlotte had been quite jealous of him: the time Eliot spent with Skip was time he did not spend with her. But since Eliot had gone to Montana and Charlotte had started working at the Bullard Farm during the summers, she'd gotten used to Skip. Under his sardonic exterior she found he was very nice. He put in long hours at the farm helping Andy, although he didn't like farm work, and he'd given Deb a great deal of practical advice and assistance with setting up the store.

It was the bank where Skip worked that had financed the Magic Cupboard. In the beginning there had been a lot of details to see to, strategies to plan, hitches to straighten out. It was natural that he would spend quite a bit of time with Deb. Two years later the business was well-established and running smoothly, and he still spent quite a bit of time with Deb . .

Chapter Six

LYING IN BED THE NEXT MORNING, CHARLOTTE WOKE UP JUST enough to hear the no-school announcements on her radio, then curled herself into a warm ball and slept until ten. Sometime during the night the snow had stopped, but the temperature dropped; and by dawn the world was frozen tight in a thick sheath of ice. Even though the road crews from the Department of Public Works had been out for hours scraping and sanding, there were many streets they hadn't got to, and the sidewalks were mostly impassible, covered with rough, rutted ice. It was strongly recommended that anyone who didn't have to go out stay home, and the news all day was full of cancellations and traffic accidents.

Mr. Paige went off to the museum mid-morning, full of gloom, to see what new disasters had occurred. He muttered about ice dams and ruined plaster, and why would *any*one want to be the administrator of *any*thing *any*way—it was a *thankless* job. Charlotte was downstairs by then, rummaging for breakfast. She and her mother exchanged glances and kept prudently silent, secure in the knowledge that they could legitimately spend the whole day at home doing whatever they liked. Mrs. Paige's contractors would certainly not come down from Lowell on a day like this.

In the afternoon, Mrs. Paige called Commodore Shattuck to ask if he and Oliver could come to dinner on Friday. She reported to Charlotte that he sounded very chipper and was delighted to accept. "He says he's developing a fierce case of

cabin fever. He claims Oliver's been bullying him unmerci-
fully—won't even let him out to bird-feed in the back yard."

"Hmmp," said Charlotte. "You ought to hear the two of
them squabbling. They sound like a couple of little kids
teasing each other. I expect the Commodore bullies right back
when he has a mind to. Was Oliver around? I meant to talk
to him about Saturday."

"He was out spreading salt on the driveway and chipping
ice off the steps. Sam's lucky to have someone handy to do
that sort of thing for him, and Oliver does seem responsible.
You know, darling," she continued, "I think it would be a
nice idea if you did something about our walk before your
father gets home."

Charlotte rolled her eyes. "Oh, all right. I should have seen
it coming. This is Oliver's fault."

By Wednesday the sidewalks were still bad, but life was
back on schedule, school chugging along as usual. This was
the time of year when you had to abandon Christmas and try
your level best to put thoughts of summer vacation out of
your mind. Of course, there was February vacation, but if
you didn't think about that, then it came like a wonderful
surprise present.

Last period on Thursday, Charlotte and Kath were together in first year French; they shared that and math. As
they shuffled into their seats, Kath said, "Isn't Oliver in school
today?"

"Of course he is. I saw him in English, third period. Why
wouldn't he be?"

"It's just he wasn't at lunch. I looked for him and he wasn't
there."

"You must have missed him, or he went to the library instead. Why did you want to see him? He knows we're going
somewhere Saturday, I told him."

Kath's face got noticeably pink, and she said with a show
of vagueness, "Oh, nothing special. I just thought—I mean,
I wondered if he was sick or something."

The bell rang, signaling the start of their next round with
the imperfect tense. The struggle required all of Charlotte's

concentration, and when class was over, Kath grabbed up her books, said a hasty goodbye, and dashed off for the gym. She had made the girls' junior varsity, which was a very good team that year. Although Charlotte had no desire to play herself, she enjoyed watching and cheering for someone she knew. Andy always went to home games when he wasn't working, and sometimes Oliver could be coaxed along. He actively disliked team sports as a participant, but he'd begun playing tennis in the eighth grade and stayed with it because he was good. He preferred individual competition.

Outside the classroom, Charlotte flattened herself against the wall and thought for a minute. Oliver's last class on Thursday was math, in the science building. It would be simpler to look for him at his locker, on the other side of Humanities, where she was now. If he wasn't there, he'd be on his bus already—he went straight home after school these days—and she'd have missed him. She joined the torrent of students and worked her way around the central core of offices and language labs to locker 392. He wasn't there, and there was no sign of him in either direction.

Wasted effort, thought Charlotte sourly, and turned back to her own locker to collect her parka and exchange some books. It didn't really matter, she had nothing special to see Oliver about. It was just that Kath's question had reminded her that, although she'd *seen* him earlier in the day, they had hardly spoken. He had almost seemed to avoid her. But some days he was like that, uncommunicative; she'd gotten used to it. The halls were beginning to clear out, leaving clots of kids here and there who were in no hurry to leave: they were walkers like Charlotte, or they had meetings, sports, detention, nothing in particular to go home for.

She found Oliver leaning against her locker door with his left shoulder, obviously waiting for her, and her spirits lifted. "Hello. Where have you been?" he asked, as if she were late for an appointment.

She almost said, "Looking for you," then thought better of it. Why be obvious? "I had to find someone," she said instead.

"And did you?" He pushed himself out of her way.

43

"Yes, as a matter of fact." She rooted through the locker. "You'll miss your bus."

"Thought I'd walk today."

She found what she wanted—her algebra book and notes. "Why?" she asked with her head inside.

"What?"

"I said, why? Here, hold these while I put on my parka."

"Wondered if you might want to stop at Friendly's for a milkshake or something."

She stared at him, one arm in the sleeve. "Don't you have to get home?"

He shrugged off-handedly. "Of course, if you don't want to—"

"I didn't say that, it's just—you don't usually—I don't think I've got very much money with me."

"You don't need any. I'm inviting you."

"Okay." She took her books back. His expression gave her no clues, it was unreadable. She would have to wait for him to tell her what was going on, though she was filled with curiosity. He was not in the habit of offering her milkshakes at Friendly's—he didn't much like Friendly's: too crowded, rowdy, and full of fried smells. She clung to her patience and reflected that a milkshake was a milkshake, no matter why it was offered, and it had been a long time since she had allowed herself one.

They walked into the windy glare of the afternoon. Charlotte clutched her books and wished she'd remembered to wear her hat; she could feel her ears starting to sting. Beside her, Oliver strode along, wrapped in his own thoughts. He was taller than she by several inches, and she had to consciously work to keep up. A couple of members of the boys' track team jogged past in maroon sweat suits, their breath fogging the air around their heads.

"Hey," said Charlotte when they reached Thoreau Street, "remember me? You asked me to come."

"Hnnh?" He glanced around.

"You don't have to talk if you don't want to, but do we have to run?"

He slowed down for a block or so, but then he forgot

44

again. Charlotte sighed and increased her speed. Friendly's, when they got there, was already full, the air warm and heavy with smells from the grill, smoke, and conversation. It was loud and cheerful. Charlotte recognized a lot of their classmates, smiled and waved at several. It felt nice, being there with someone—being there with Oliver. In junior high, she had been intimidated by her contemporaries. She hadn't known any of them very well, or cared to. Her brother Eliot had been her best, really her only, friend. She loved him very much, and he had taught her a great deal, but she'd come to realize, since he'd left Concord, that in a certain sense he had made things harder for her by being such a good friend. She had depended too much on one person and had excluded other possibilities. It was a hard thing to learn; she'd passed through hurt, anger, resentment when he'd left, but she thought she was out on the other side now. And she had other friends.

She and Oliver stood by the door looking for two empty places. There were a couple of vacant stools at the counter. She nudged him and pointed, but he shook his head, so they waited for a booth. It was his money so she couldn't complain. Eventually two older women got up to leave; it took them several minutes to collect their belongings, arrange scarves, straighten coats, smooth gloves. They had a short discussion over the tip, then at last they were gone, and Oliver dodged in to claim the booth before anyone else could.

"That's better." He took the menu and studied it. Charlotte didn't bother. When their frazzled, pink-faced waitress came, she ordered a double-thick chocolate milkshake. Oliver frowned indecisively, then made up his mind. "A cheeseburger with lettuce and tomato, french fries, and a cup of cocoa."

Charlotte's eyes widened in amazement. "Kath said she didn't see you at lunch today—didn't you have anything at all to eat?"

"Is she keeping track of me?" He scowled. "No. I wasn't hungry. I did some homework instead."

"English project," she guessed.

"What? No, not yet." He sank into a broody silence.

Charlotte propped her chin on her hand. She could feel

45

depression settling gently around them like a fog. "Mother saw a house she likes yesterday," she said finally. "I'm supposed to go and see it with her tomorrow after school."

"Oh?" said Oliver without much interest.

"She's really enthusiastic about this one—it's the first time. Out beyond you, off Monument Street. Ball's Hill. At least we'd be on the same bus."

Oliver gave her an odd, sharp look.

"Chocolate milkshake? And cocoa." The waitress set them down at the wrong places and darted away. Charlotte exchanged the cup and saucer gladly for the two glasses of lovely thick brown stuff. In spite of the gloominess, she gazed at them with a quiet sort of rapture. In a peculiar way, she was grateful for Deb's persistent nagging about junk food and sugar. Although it was true that Charlotte had lost a lot of her puppy fat and was developing a respectable figure, the bonus was that she actually enjoyed forbidden things like chocolate much more than she ever used to because she didn't get them very often. She used to buy a candy bar whenever she felt the slightest need for cheering up, now she had to be really desperate for one.

"Well." Oliver blew the steam off the top of his cup and shook himself out of whatever he was thinking about. "You do live in an enormous house, I mean for the three of you."

"That's what everyone says," said Charlotte. "But it's where I've always lived. It's home."

His eyes narrowed. "You shouldn't get so attached to a place. It's only walls and a roof. Not worth it. You won't be leaving Concord, after all."

"I know. And I'm pretty resigned to it, actually. But I have trouble thinking about strange people moving into our house and changing everything around—painting the bathrooms different colors, not taking care of Eliot's daffodils and tulips, putting the beds in the wrong places. How would *you* feel if it was the Commodore's house?"

He glanced at her, then quickly away, as the waitress zipped back with his cheeseburger and fries. "Anything else?"

"Ketchup, please."

"You don't use ketchup," said Charlotte.

46

"This afternoon I want ketchup. Do you mind?" He spent quite a long time spreading it on his cheeseburger and arranging it to his satisfaction. He seemed in no hurry to go anywhere. In fact, as they sat there, Charlotte noticed that he was taking an unusually long time over everything. He ate very slowly, chewing each bite with great thoroughness and pausing before the next, wiping his fingers, stirring his cocoa. Something was oppressing him and she didn't think he was getting any closer to telling her what it was, but she was convinced that was why he'd asked her here.

She made up her mind. "Are you worried about something?"

"What?" He sounded genuinely surprised. "Why should I be?"

"I don't know. I'm asking. Do you want to tell me what's bothering you?"

"How do you know—" he began, then stopped and said, "No," emphatically. "At least not yet. I'm not sure—I haven't made up my mind."

"I can't make this milkshake last much longer."

"Have another one."

She snorted. "I'd explode. Or be sick. Probably be sick."

"Have some french fries then. I don't like them."

"I didn't think you did. Look, Oliver, you must want to tell me, or you wouldn't have suggested this. Is it so awful?"

He wouldn't look at her. "About as bad as it can be," he said quietly. "I don't know what to do. I thought if I gave myself time I could work it out, but I can't. They're not going to let me handle it, I know they aren't."

"They?" She was mystified, but watching him she felt a small cold place grow in the pit of her stomach. What? School? No, it couldn't be; he was doing well. He was on the Honor Roll. When he finished high school, he had decided he would go to Harvard, and Charlotte didn't doubt he would. She didn't think "they" could be the Commodore, either. It had to be his parents. It must have something to do with his abortive Christmas trip—one of his parents must be making trouble. She guessed it was his mother—his father seemed to have vanished from his life virtually altogether,

47

gone to California, where he was dean of some university or other. But what? Tentatively she suggested, "Maybe my parents can help. Your mother talks to mine, you know."

"My mother? Oh lord." He groaned, then abruptly began to pull on his jacket.

"Oliver—"

"Come on, let's get out of here. This is no good."

He hadn't finished anything: cheeseburger, fries, cocoa. Her milkshake glasses were both empty. He clapped a handful of change onto the table, and while he paid the bill, she piled her books together. Outdoors the icy air made her shiver. "Where are we going?"

"I don't know," he said angrily. "Can we go to your house?"

"Well—yes. Sure. But what about the Commodore? Won't he wonder where you are? You're more than an hour late. Won't he worry?"

At the corner outside the liquor store, Oliver stopped and faced her. His guard was down, he looked confused and exposed, and she was frightened. "He's not going to worry. At all. Ever again. Charlotte, he's dead."

Her mouth opened and nothing came out of it.

Chapter Seven

THEY STOOD MOTIONLESS, STARING AT EACH OTHER. CHARLOTTE was blank; Oliver's words entered her ears meaninglessly. But they drilled relentlessly into her brain like an auger, penetrating deeper and deeper until they must make sense. Oliver began to walk then, very quickly, in the direction of Charlotte's house, as if by hurrying he could leave the words behind, like vapor to disperse in the cold air. He was quite far ahead before she could make her legs work to follow.

"Wait!" she called after him. "Wait a minute, Oliver!"

He didn't stop until he reached the traffic lights. When she caught up and saw his face wrenched with misery, the words finally broke through and she shivered violently, chilled from the inside this time. They crossed the street. There was no one home, Charlotte had known there wouldn't be. She used her key in the back door and led the way into the kitchen. Automatically she turned on the light and turned up the thermostat by the stairs. Oliver sat at the table. From the cellar came the reassuring grumble of the furnace. She thought, good, I will feel warm again, put down her books and sat across from him. "Oliver," she said in a small voice, "how do you know?"

He had regained control of himself. "What do you mean, how do I know? I wouldn't say it if I wasn't sure."

"But how do you know he's—" She couldn't utter the word.

"Dead." He said it flatly. "He's stopped breathing. His heart doesn't beat. He was quite cold this morning."

49

She gazed at him in horror. "This morning?" she whispered.

"I was sure last night," Oliver went on dispassionately. "When I went to bed. But there wasn't anything I could do—there didn't seem to be any point in getting everyone stirred up. I thought maybe by morning I'd have worked something out. Look, Charlotte," he said in answer to her expression, "it was after eleven and no one could help Uncle Sam. He was gone."

"You knew and you stayed there?"

"Oh, for God's sake, Charlotte!" he said angrily. "What difference did it make? He's my great-uncle. He didn't die of anything contagious, it wasn't violent—he just went to sleep—it was very peaceful. I don't think he even knew it was happening. It was just as if he wasn't there anymore, as if he'd gone away. It was just me and—" He broke off and closed his eyes. "Oh, hell. I forgot. I have to go back, right now." He stood up and buttoned his jacket. "*Stupid!*" he said fiercely.

Alarmed, she said, "What do you mean? Why?"

"Amos, of course. He's been inside since I left for school. I've got to go back to him."

"He could wait a little longer." Charlotte thought desperately ahead to when her parents would get home. This was for them, not her, to deal with.

"He'll have to go out," said Oliver implacably. "And he needs me—he hates being by himself."

She knew by then that it was real, that it was happening, but she couldn't help thinking if only she could wake up. The sun would be stretched thin across the end of the afternoon, the world would be steady, the whole thing would blow away like the tatters of a dream. The idea of going to Commodore Shattuck's house filled her with a clammy dread. But Oliver was heading for the door and she couldn't let him go alone. She didn't want to stay in her own house by herself either, not now that she knew.

Her feelings must have been plain on her face, because he said, "It's all right. You don't have to come."

But she knew she did.

It was nearly four; the stunted winter afternoon was ebbing

toward night and already the traffic was thickening on Main Street. Behind the store and office windows lay light and people. As they walked through the center of town, Charlotte thought longingly of Deb waiting on customers, Skip sitting at a desk. Either one of them could help; they would be brisk and adult and comforting, they would release the two of them from the awful burden of being the only ones who knew. It would take only a few extra minutes to find Deb or Skip, to blurt the news. But with a sidelong glance at Oliver, she knew better than to suggest it. He had chosen to tell her, not because she would know what to do and whom to go to, she realized, but out of some other need.

Charlotte had forgotten how far it was to the Commodore's house on foot. Normally she bicycled. And this year, gloriously, there were cars. She was too young for a license or a learner's permit, but Oliver and Andy had licenses—Kath still preferred horses. It had opened up a whole new range of possibilities and independence.

Out Monument Street, the air was seasoned with wood smoke, and there were lights on over front doors and in front rooms; people were waiting inside, for their families to come home, thinking about supper, what they would talk about, what the evening held. It was all calm and normal, just as it had been yesterday and would be tomorrow. It didn't seem possible to Charlotte that Commodore Shattuck could be dead and nothing look different.

The word kept floating away from her, like a balloon too big to grasp. Maybe he wasn't. She was simply going with Oliver to his house for supper, to do homework, to visit his great-uncle, nothing out of the ordinary. They'd cross the river, and tucked in next to it on the right would be the little gray house, a light over the front door, waiting for them, Amos prancing and wagging and making a nuisance of himself. The Commodore would look up from his book with his familiar fierce smile and say it was about time, he was beginning to feel hollow. It would be Oliver's fault if he fainted dead away one of these days while his great-nephew was out gallivanting. They'd sit in the living room, listening to *All Things Considered* on the radio because the Commodore detested the gratuitous sensationalism of television news—"Who wants to see bodies carried out of burning houses and blood all over the street?" Oliver refused to watch the national news; his stepfather was Washington correspondent for one of the major networks and appeared regularly. Charlotte's parents watched him, and so sometimes did she, out of curiosity. Privately, she thought he was rather impressive, though she felt sure she wouldn't want to be related to him.

While Charlotte and Oliver drank V-8 or cranapple juice, Commodore Shattuck would allow himself what he called a tot of bourbon and water—more water than bourbon, Oliver would see to that. He'd ask what they'd done at school all day, and if they thought it was worthwhile—no one else asked if they thought school was worthwhile. He'd inquire about Charlotte's family and bring out his most recent letter from his Scottish friend, Jimmy MacPherson, even if it was the same one Charlotte had heard the last time. It didn't matter, though Oliver would frown.

It seemed as if she had always known Commodore Shattuck, had always been friends with Oliver and Andy and Kath. It had actually been not quite three years, but three years was long to her: it was one fifth of her life. What were three years to someone who was eighty-two? For something measured so precisely, time had the most peculiar way of warping and shifting.

Charlotte had slipped so far away into her thoughts that it was a nasty shock when they actually did cross the ice-scarred river and confront the dark house huddled beside the bridge. She looked at it and knew with a sudden plunging of the stomach that it was empty. Unlike hers, it shouldn't have been. Somewhere within it was a dead person. She had never seen a dead person, never been in a house with one, never even been to a funeral. She shivered.

Oliver went right up the side steps, opened the door to the kitchen, and thrust into the darkness. Instantly Amos was tumbling around their knees, licking every scrap of bare skin he could find in ecstasy. Oliver bent and gave him a hard, swift hug and he whimpered in delight.

For once Charlotte was genuinely glad to see Amos. She

52

reached out and took a handful of his rough, thick fur, felt him vibrate with life under her fingers, and drew courage from him. Her heart steadied and she followed Oliver inside. "Oliver," she said in a voice that was nearly normal, "where is he?"

Oliver turned on the light and rinsed and refilled Amos's water dish. The kitchen was tidy as usual, nothing out of place. If Oliver had eaten breakfast this morning, he had washed and put away the dishes afterward. "I'll get his leash. It's in the hall," he said.

She bit her lip. Commodore Shattuck could be anywhere—in the front room where she'd seen him last, in the dining room where Oliver did his homework, upstairs. He might be sitting in a chair or lying on the floor—perhaps he'd fallen on the stairs, the way his old friend Ophelia Wardlaw had. She hadn't died, she'd broken her hip. Charlotte was trapped—she didn't dare leave the kitchen for fear of what she might find. Panic constricted her throat, making it hard to swallow.

But Oliver was back in a minute with the long leather training leash in one hand. "You don't have to look so stricken," he said matter-of-factly. "He can't do you any harm. He's upstairs, in his own bed. If you saw him you'd probably think he was asleep."

She couldn't keep from asking, "Are you sure he isn't?"

He gave her a scornful look, clipped the leash onto Amos's collar, then said slowly and empatically, "Uncle Sam is dead. Wishing isn't going to change a thing, Charlotte. It just gets in the way of finding a solution."

"A solution? To what?"

"To what I'm going to do next. I have to decide."

She blinked at him, trying to understand. "Where are you going now?"

"To take Amos out," he said impatiently. "I told you. Just a short walk," he said to the eager dog. Amos was dancing from paw to paw.

"I'm coming too," said Charlotte hastily. Oliver made no comment.

They walked back over the bridge to the entrance of the North Bridge park, a dark tunnel under high, bare trees. Snow

53

glimmered in the fields on either side. Amos behaved surprisingly well on his leash; he made a mighty effort to hold himself to Oliver's pace, stopped when Oliver stopped, and sat on the frozen ground until Oliver went on. When he forgot, Oliver automatically reminded him with a word or a short jerk on the leash. When Amos succeeded there was a quick pat. They were going to dog school together. Charlotte had been to a couple of chaotic classes at the beginning. Oliver had not encouraged her to keep visiting, and all those dogs had oppressed her. It had appeared then that Amos had no aptitude at all for obedience training, just a slobbery good will toward all and a bumbling, insatiable curiosity about the other students. But Oliver persevered: Tuesday nights were dog school. And Amos had obviously learned a great deal.

At the bottom of the path, the bridge arched its back over the cold river. They walked up it to the middle, their boots making dull, hollow thuds on the wooden planks. The day had sunk to a hard, bright rim at the edge of the sky behind the black fringe of trees. The sound of home-bound cars came clear through the sharp, still air.

"Well, you can't stay there," said Charlotte, leaning her elbows on the rail. She felt calmer away from the house.

"No, once people know they won't let me," he agreed grimly. "But I haven't told anyone except you, and until to-morrow—"

"Oliver, no!"

"Don't make a fuss," he exclaimed. "I thought you wouldn't."

"I'm not. I just don't see how you can stay in that house another night with a—with the Commodore—that way."

"With a corpse, you mean."

She pulled her arms tight around her and bent over the water, her hair falling forward.

"It isn't Uncle Sam, Charlotte," said Oliver in a minute. "It's only what's left of him. He went upstairs after supper last night, said he was tired and wanted to rest his eyes. When I finished the dishes I went to check—I had to get some books anyway—and he was asleep with his quilt up. I didn't hear him again, so when I went to bed, I looked in to turn off his light. He was lying just the same way, but he was different. I could feel it. He'd gone. That's all. He didn't even cry out when it happened. He didn't wake up. He just died." His tone was flat, final, allowing for no other possibilities. "There isn't a smell, you know."

"I never—" protested Charlotte. "That's not at *all*—"

"What's the problem? That's where I live. What am I supposed to do—beat it out of there and check into the Colonial Inn?" he asked angrily. "What do you think people used to do with dead bodies before there were funeral homes?"

She didn't know what to say; she couldn't look at him. The conversation was fantastically macabre—part of her couldn't believe they were having it. He was so cold-blooded about it. But she noticed his right hand—he hadn't worn his gloves—his fingers clenched tight around Amos's leash. Pulling her wits together, she said, "I'm not—I've never thought about any of this before. I'm sorry. But you've got to tell someone, Oliver, not just me. I don't know what to do. It—it isn't right just to leave him there, like that."

"I *know*," he said in a tight, thin voice. "I have no intention of leaving him. All I need is enough time to sort myself out. As soon as I tell people they'll take over. Everything, not just Uncle Sam. I'm not legally old enough—I'll lose control, and it won't matter what *I* want to do, only what they think's good for me."

"But you couldn't keep it secret much longer anyway," she pointed out practically. "You and the Commodore are supposed to come to dinner tomorrow night. If you called Mom and said he wasn't well—" a thought struck her. "Oliver, did you know? I mean, when you came back right after Christmas, was it—?"

"Of course I didn't. You saw him then, he was perfectly all right. Do you think I wouldn't have said something if he wasn't? Do you think his doctor wouldn't have known? Do you?" he demanded.

She shook her head.

"All right then." He heaved a great weary sigh. "Heel, Amos. Let's go home."

He walked quickly, shoulders hunched. Charlotte wished she could take his hand, put her arm through his, touch him; for comfort, for reassurance, for them both, but he did not invite contact. As she hurried along beside him, she tried to sort out her feelings, tried to find the grief and sense of loss that ought to be there. The Commodore's dead, she told herself over and over, the Commodore's dead. But she could identify neither. Surely she ought to feel more than a kind of horror and revulsion at the idea of Oliver inhabiting the same house as his great-uncle's body.

Chapter Eight

"ANYWAY," SAID OLIVER, AS HE FIXED AMOS'S SUPPER, "I'M NOT keeping it secret. I haven't lied to anyone. I'm not going to bury him in the back yard and pretend he's still alive. I've just—oh, skip it."

Amos sat high on his haunches, ears cocked, watching intently as Oliver mixed cottage cheese, carrot, meat scraps, and dog food in his dish.

"Eats as well as any person in Concord, that dog." Charlotte could hear the Commodore saying it in his dry, gruff voice, as clearly as if he'd been standing at her elbow. A bitter-tasting lump rose in her throat. "Tell my parents, Oliver," she said urgently. "They can take care of things. They'll know what to do."

"*I* know what to do," said Oliver.

She shook her head with conviction. "The longer you wait, the worse it'll get. People won't understand why you didn't do something right away—as soon as it happened. They won't. It'll be awful. You *have* to tell them tonight. If you don't, I will."

His eyes narrowed dangerously. "It isn't your business."

"Yes, it is," she argued passionately. "He's—he was a friend of mine. And so are you. And you made it my business when you told me."

Amos gave a frustrated little yip, blowing through his whiskers, and Oliver set the dish on the floor next to his water bowl. Amos plunged his gray muzzzle into it with pleasure;

tiny blobs of cottage cheese splattered the linoleum.

Oliver stood against her stubbornly, countering her arguments with unyielding silence. Amos cleaned his bowl and chased it across the floor, polishing it obsessively with his long, eager tongue. The telephone rang, startling them both. Oliver unhooked the receiver. "Hello? Yes? Oh, yes. Yes, she is. Just a minute, please." His voice was even and polite, betraying nothing.

"Who is it?" whispered Charlotte in alarm.

"Your mother." He handed her the phone, retrieved Amos's dish, and went to rinse it. Amos raised his eyebrows and flattened his ears sadly, seeing the end of another supper.

"Hello?" Charlotte wondered how her mother could possibly have guessed about Commodore Shattuck, but of course she hadn't. She was merely calling to find out where Charlotte was and when she'd be home, and to point out a little briskly that it would have been nice of her to leave a note. Charlotte said she was sorry and, watching Oliver's back, asked quickly if it would be all right to bring him home for supper. She saw him stiffen and willed her mother to agree without discussion.

"Well, I guess so, darling. He *is* coming tomorrow night, you remember. And what about Sam?"

"He's out," blurted Charlotte. "We came to feed Amos."

"Out?" Her mother sounded doubtful. "But he—well, never mind. Just come straight home. I've got a casserole in the oven and it'll dry out if you're late."

Oliver said nothing when she hung up. In silence they buttoned and zipped themselves into their jackets, and he put Amos back on his leash. "I'm not going to leave him here," he said in answer to Charlotte's frown. "He's been alone all day. We'll take the car."

"Do you think we should?"

"Why not? Uncle Sam isn't going to use it," he snapped. He left the lights on over the sink and outside the back door, even though they both knew he was unlikely to be back that night.

Charlotte went to stand at the edge of the road, to watch for traffic, as Oliver backed the car out. The driveway was largely hidden from oncoming cars by the bridge parapets, and it was the Commodore's rule that there should always be a lookout. She was quite unprepared for the lancing pain in her chest as she saw the taillights slide toward her.

She had hardly been aware that Oliver was learning to drive last year. He never said anything about getting a learner's permit; she saw it in his wallet once when he was looking for his library card.

"When did you get that?" she asked in surprise. Learner's permits were brandished as badges of distinction around the high school.

Off-handedly he replied, "Oh, several weeks ago."

"Have you actually been driving?"

He shrugged dismissively. "A bit."

"But you never said! Is it fun? Are you taking lessons? You aren't in driver ed., are you?"

"No," he said, and wouldn't tell her any more, in typical Oliver fashion, though she found out from the Commodore he was taking lessons at a driving school. Nor would he agree to let her come when he practiced. "Wait until I have my license," he said flatly. As with everything he set his mind to, he studied hard and learned quickly, not because he liked the process of learning, but because he wanted to get it over with as soon and unobtrusively as possible.

Andy was just the opposite. He made no secret of his progress from learner to full-fledged driver, but for him it was hardly a brand-new skill he was learning; he'd been driving since he was eleven, only on the farm, of course. But he already knew all about gears and the clutch and backing up. The difficult part for him was the written test and memorizing the laws in the pink booklet. Tests in general made him freeze, and this was no different. For weeks that booklet lived in his back pocket getting more and more tattered and grubby, and whenever he had a spare moment with anyone he would pull it out and make his long-suffering companion quiz him. Charlotte had never seen Oliver with a copy.

Early one Saturday in September, some six months after his sixteenth birthday, Oliver had appeared unexpectedly at the Paiges' front door and asked for Charlotte.

Mr. Paige, who answered the doorbell, gave him a peculiar

look and ambled out to the kitchen where Charlotte was sitting in her sweat shirt robe eating waffles and reading *Gone With the Wind*.

"Charlie," said her father, "it's for you."

She looked up blankly from the siege of Atlanta. "Humm?"

"There's a young man at the front door for you."

"A young man? What? Who is it?"

"I'm not quite sure. He looks vaguely familiar, but he's acting very strangely, and I think he's got wheels."

"What *are* you talking about? I'm not dressed. Who would come this early? Didn't you ask him who he is and what he wants?"

"He wants you," said her father imperturbably, sitting down again to his coffee and the sports section of the Boston *Globe*.

She gave him a hard, suspicious look. "I smell a rat somewhere." Irritably, she stuffed a double bite of syrupy waffle into her mouth and went to see what her father was babbling about.

"Good morning," said Oliver. "I came by to see if you were interested in going to Acton with me. I have to get sunflower seed for Uncle Sam."

"Acton. Sunflower seed? What's going on?"

"I'll wait while you get dressed," he offered blandly. "Or at least put on some shoes." He studied her with a grin. "You look like a green bean in that. It's quite becoming in its way."

"Oliver Shattuck, you're out of your mind. It isn't even nine a.m., it's chilly and wet out there, and I'm in the middle of my breakfast. Why in the world would I want to go to Acton to buy birdseed with you?"

"I thought you might like the ride. I'm driving."

"But—" The light broke. "*You're* driving? Oliver, have you *got* it? Have you really?"

"Of course I have. I wouldn't be here asking you to go along with me otherwise."

"Just us? You and me?"

"I don't have a cheering squad in the back seat."

"But you never said! Aren't you excited? That's neat! I'll

be ready in a few minutes. You go and talk to Dad while I change."

"I thought he seemed familiar," remarked Mr. Paige as they came in. "But the light at the front door makes people look different. I seldom recognize 'em when they come in that way. Toast yourself a waffle, Oliver, and tell me what you think of the Celtics. Are they going to make it, or fade at the last minute again?"

"No thank you, I've had breakfast. I just came—"

"We're going to Acton, Dad," Charlotte interrupted him.

"Wow," said her father politely.

"No, he's got his driver's license, Daddy! Isn't that great?"

"Ah. First step on the road to becoming a commuter. Congratulations," said Mr. Paige. "You didn't waste much time about it, Oliver, aren't you just old enough? That's what I thought." He looked at his daughter who was about to disappear up the back stairs. "Next it'll be you, I suppose. Good lord. Car insurance, bigger gas bills, extra sets of keys—" She escaped.

Predictably, Oliver drove well. He observed traffic signs and speed limits, signaled each turn, knew without hesitation which switch worked the windshield wipers, which key opened the hatch when they loaded the seed. He made no mistakes on the way to the grain mill or back. Charlotte was impressed. It was only later, and through a remark made by the Commodore, that she discovered he had actually done a trial run before he asked her along. Once it would have infuriated her, but this time she didn't even let on she knew. He hadn't done it so much to show off as to save himself the embarrassment of making mistakes in front of her. She thought she was being commendably mature.

Andy wasn't exactly careless by comparison. He drove competently as long as he kept his mind on the road in front and the traffic around. But when he began to think about fertilizer, for instance, how much and when to spread it, he lost track of what he was doing. The farm was always there in his head, no matter what else was going on.

They were so dissimilar, Andy and Oliver. Andy was open

61

and direct, easy to read because he didn't disguise his feelings or hide his obsession with the farm. Most of Oliver was hidden most of the time. It was dangerously easy to take Andy for granted, but Oliver was too unpredictable.

As she climbed into the car beside Oliver, Charlotte tried to put Andy in his place. What would Andy have done about Commodore Shattuck? He wouldn't have kept quiet about him for twenty-four hours for a start, she was sure of that. Even if he hadn't said anything, it would have showed all over his face. But Oliver had gone to bed, gotten up and had breakfast, gone to school, *knowing* and not saying a word about it to anyone. Until he told her. And why her? She couldn't do anything about it herself. What had he expected?

"This is the right thing," she said as firmly as she could. "Really it is, Oliver. You'll see. They'll know how to handle everything." She yearned toward her parents; she didn't want to have to cope, she was glad not to be old enough. This was dangerous, unfamiliar territory; if she and Oliver were forced to enter it, she wanted someone experienced to take responsibility.

Oliver swung into the driveway and parked beyond the garage. He looked at her as he cut the engine; it was not a grateful, relieved sort of look. "Where can I put Amos? It's too cold to leave him in the car."

"What about the sunporch," she suggested. "There won't be any cats out there."

She went in through the kitchen while Oliver took Amos to the porch door to wait for her to open it. Her parents were there, in the kitchen, discussing something. They stopped when she appeared, in the way that usually meant they'd been talking about her.

"There you are," said Mr. Paige. "We were about to send out the search cats."

Mrs. Paige gave her an inquiring glance. "Where's Oliver, darling? Didn't he come after all?"

"Yes, he came, but he brought Amos. We're going to shut him on the sunporch."

"Amos? The dog? But why on earth—?"

"We'll be right in." She ducked out of the room without

explaining. The dining room table was set for four, as if Oliver had been expected all along instead of invited at the last minute. He and Amos were outside the glass door, their breath making clouds. Amos greeted her as if he hadn't seen her before that day, wagging and muttering and prancing clumsily. If only he didn't try so hard, she thought irritably, he'd be easier to like.

"I didn't say anything, but they know something's up because of Amos," she warned Oliver. "I don't see why you had to bring him, if you left him in the house all day—"

"Because," said Oliver grimly, "once they know, they won't let me stay there. They aren't going to let me go back again tonight, and I wouldn't leave Amos there on his own."

"But—"

"Look, Charlotte, it's already out of my control. Don't you understand that?"

Distressed, she said, "Oliver, I'm sorry, but what else is there to do? I'd have thought you'd be glad to hand it over to someone. Are you mad at me?"

He bent and pulled gently at Amos's gray-felt ear, reminding her of his great-uncle. "I don't know what I am. Amos, you stay. Sit and *stay*."

Amos gave him a tragic look as if to say, "You can't mean it!" but he sat on his haunches. "Good dog," said Oliver, and the stringy tail flickered.

"He won't try to get out, will he? Because it's a strange place?" Charlotte asked as they shut the door on him.

"Of course not. I've told him to stay, haven't I? He knows what it means." He caught her arm suddenly and made her turn to look at him. "Promise—you let me do this. All right? Promise."

She nodded. His hand was being forced, but he'd wanted it to happen, otherwise he never would have come back with her. She couldn't have made him. He hated it, but he could think of no better alternative.

It was agonizing to sit there at dinner, knowing what she knew and her parents didn't, waiting for Oliver to choose his moment, wondering when it would come and what he would say. The blood throbbed in her ears, and she found it almost impossible to eat anything. The conversation had worked around to her father's museum and the problem he was having finding volunteers to fill in where he couldn't afford staff. "They're so damned unreliable," he said crossly. "Always going off to Bermuda or Arizona and forgetting to mention it until two days before. It eats up all my time, sorting out piddling details, making sure everything's covered. *I* oughtn't to have to do it."

"But you handle them so well, darling. You know you do. You get far more work out of them than Roger Keller ever did."

"I'm sick to death of it," said Mr. Paige grumpily.

"What about high school students?" asked Oliver, as if he had nothing else on his mind. "Through the art department. There are clubs for everything else you can think of. Mr. Ianelli'd be willing to organize something for you, I bet. Internships."

"Umm," grunted Mr. Paige. "I need intelligent people with a sense of responsibility, not a bunch of kids playing games."

"Just a thought," said Oliver.

"It might be worth looking into," said Mrs. Paige. "What do you think, Charlotte?"

"What?" She'd been listening to their voices floating around her without paying attention to the words.

"Darling, are you feeling all right?" Her mother looked at her with concern. "You've hardly touched your pork."

"I've got a headache, that's all." She was aware of Oliver, sitting very still across the table from her.

"I hope you aren't coming down with 'flu. There's an intestinal one going through the workmen right now—we're going to be weeks behind. How's your great-uncle, Oliver? Charlotte said he'd gone out tonight?" It sounded like a casual question, but the silence that followed it was not casual. Charlotte sensed that both her parents were waiting for the answer. Her stomach knotted.

Oliver told them in a flat, unemotional voice. Charlotte saw the lines between her mother's eyebrows deepen swiftly from question to shock. Her father's expression went from irritable to grave. Just as Charlotte had, he asked, "Are you sure?"

64

"Yes," said Oliver. "He died last night."

"Last night? But why didn't you let us know at once? It didn't matter how late it was, you could have called," said Mrs. Paige.

"You couldn't have done anything. There didn't seem to be any reason to upset everyone. It wouldn't have helped Uncle Sam."

Charlotte's parents exchanged a glance. "Who's his doctor?" asked Mr. Paige then in a calm, sensible voice. He was taking over. Charlotte felt an enormous sense of relief.

"Culhane," said Oliver, giving in. "Do you have to call him now?"

"He's got to know. He'll have to verify it. The sooner the better, I'd say." Mr. Paige got up. "If you'll excuse me, I'll see if I can get hold of him. Is the house locked?"

Oliver nodded.

"Then we'll need the key."

"I'll go with you."

"Oliver, why don't you stay here and let Gordon and Dennis Culhane take care of this right now?" said Mrs. Paige.

See? Oliver's eyes said to Charlotte. What did I tell you? "My clothes are all there. My school books."

"You can borrow enough to get by tonight. I'll find you some of Eliot's old pajamas, and I'm sure we've got a spare toothbrush. We'll worry about everything else tomorrow. You've got Amos with you."

He didn't argue. They sat in silence around the table, waiting for Mr. Paige to return. Charlotte's mind was empty, washed clean, like a blackboard waiting to be written over. When he came back, her father said, "Dr. Culhane's on the phone. He'd like to speak to you, Oliver. I told him I'd meet him at the house in twenty minutes."

When Oliver had gone, Mr. Paige rubbed a hand across his jaw. "What a thing."

"We ought to have seen it coming," said Mrs. Paige. "It was bound to, of course, but I spoke to Sam Tuesday about dinner tomorrow and he sounded fine. I'd never have guessed there was anything wrong."

"Culhane said there probably wasn't. Said he was out to the

house last week, just to check. Sam was taking his medicine, keeping warm, doing all the right things. His heart must have failed—no warning. He's lucky to have gone that way, I must say. I only hope I do."

Mrs. Paige frowned at him. "Charlotte, you saw Sam Sunday—"

"And I told you he was all right," she said defensively. "Oliver would have done something if he hadn't been, anyway."

"Of course he would have, Kit. And Dennis has had his eye on Sam. He didn't sound terribly surprised when I told him, just sorry. How old was he anyway? Eighty-six?"

"Eighty-two," said Charlotte, and suddenly the whole afternoon crashed down on her. She saw it explode behind her eyes. She took a gasping breath and burst into tears. Mrs. Paige left her chair and knelt, putting her arms around her. "Oh, darling, it's all right. Shhh, Charlotte. There, sweetie, there." She rocked her gently, and Charlotte cried and cried, unable to stop. She had no clear idea of what she was crying for—the Commodore, she supposed. He was the one who had died.

Chapter Nine

OLIVER CAME BACK, VERY SELF-CONTAINED, AND HER FATHER went away again, this time out into the night, and Charlotte's tears subsided, leaving her feeling swollen and shaken. Oliver had returned to his chair and was gazing absently at an oil painting on the wall, ignoring her completely. She was ashamed and resentful; how could he be so unemotional? Why hadn't he been the one to burst into tears?

"Well," said Mrs. Paige briskly, "there's no point in sitting here any longer. Charlotte, will you help clear the table? What about Amos, has he been fed?"

When Oliver didn't answer, Charlotte said yes. They all carried dishes out to the kitchen. Mrs. Paige put the leftovers away while Oliver rinsed and Charlotte filled the dishwasher. It was so confusingly ordinary: just what they would do on a normal evening, but it wasn't a normal evening. It was all wrong, but Charlotte didn't know what would have been right.

Once they'd finished, Oliver said abruptly, "I promised Amos a proper walk. He needs it—he's been inside all day."

"Do you want company?" said Mrs. Paige. "Charlotte, why don't you go along."

Oliver shook his head. "I'll just take Amos. I don't know when we'll be back."

Mrs. Paige gave him a considering look, but only said, "We'll leave the porch door open for you. Turn the lock when you come in, will you? I think we'll shut the cats in

67

here tonight. They know there's an intruder—Hu Kwah disappeared as soon as I opened the back door, and Lap is ready to go off like a rocket."

"I'll need a blanket for Amos to sleep on," said Oliver.

"Why don't you take him upstairs with you when you go to bed? He won't feel so forlorn," Mrs. Paige said. "I'll hunt up some pj's for you and you can have Eliot's room—the bed's fresh."

"He is housebroken, I hope?" Mrs. Paige said when Oliver'd gone.

"Of course he is, long ago."

"I suppose Oliver's all right, going out by himself. Maybe you should have gone along, darling."

"He didn't want me to, you heard him. He's not going to throw himself into the river or anything like that, Mom, if you're worried."

"No," Mrs. Paige agreed doubtfully. "That's not Oliver's style, is it. It's just—" She hesitated. "You're sure he will come back?"

"Yes." She was sure. He might not like handing things over to other people this way, but he was resigned to it. Besides, where would he go except to the Commodore's house, and her father and Dr. Culhane were there. Even after they left, it would be the first place people would look for him if he disappeared. Oliver was far too clever not to have worked it all out.

"What about you, darling. Are you all right now?"

She nodded. "I guess. What happens next?"

"Well." Mrs. Paige ran her fingers through her short gray hair. "Arrangements for the burial and a memorial service, I suppose. We'll have to take care of that—talk to the minister. Sam was an Episcopalian, wasn't he. I'll have to call Oliver's mother, but I'll wait until Gordon gets home before I do that. What about Oliver's father? He's Sam's relative, isn't he, not Paula?"

"Yes, but I don't know where he is except California. Oliver hardly ever says anything about him. I don't even know if they write to each other."

"California's a big state. Not very helpful. I'll let Paula

handle that, she can decide what to do about him. Then there's the house. Glory! Just thinking about it makes me tired. There aren't any other relatives that you know of, are there?" Mrs. Paige led the way up the back stairs.

"Not that I've heard about. Just friends."

"Of course, the friends will have to be told, the close ones at any rate."

"What do you mean, the house?"

Mrs. Paige opened the drawers in Eliot's bureau, one after the other, until she found what she wanted in the third one. "Goodness, he's left a lot of stuff here. These should do." She shook out a pair of bright striped flannel pajamas. "The house has to be cleaned, the contents disposed of, electricity, water, telephone shut off, someone'll have to put it on the market."

Charlotte stared at her. "Sell it, you mean?" she asked in disbelief.

"You can't expect it to sit there empty, darling. It must be worth quite a lot of money. Who would take care of it and pay the taxes? Charlotte, I know it's a shock—"

"But, I thought, Oliver—"

"He's only sixteen, my love. He can't stay there by himself, you see that. I expect he'll go back to Washington with Paula after the funeral."

Her mother was sympathetic and sensible. Charlotte couldn't think of anything to say. She hadn't considered beyond the present. It was as if someone had heaved an enormous boulder into a pond: the splash it made was so loud she hadn't begun to think about the ripples that would inevitably spread out from it.

Soon after eight Mr. Paige came home. Oliver was not yet back with Amos. Charlotte and her mother were in the living room, pretending to watch television, both of them listening for a car or the click of a door latch. Mr. Paige, looking somber, poured himself a glass of scotch before sinking onto the couch. "Everything seems to be in order," he said after a couple of swallows. "Sam was lying in bed, just as Oliver said, very peaceful. Culhane doesn't think he felt anything at all. I called the Gilbert Funeral Home and they'll take care of the arrangements for burial. It seemed to me, under the circumstances, it'd better be done right away. It's already been twenty-four hours almost."

Mrs. Paige gave her head a little shake. "Did Dennis say anything about that?"

"Not really. Just that he couldn't have done anything if Oliver had called him last night. Still, it's a bit bizarre to let it go." He glanced at Charlotte, then back to his drink. "Frank Gilbert says Sam bought himself a plot in Sleepy Hollow several years ago, so that's settled."

Sleepy Hollow. Charlotte knew it well. A green, wooded place where Eliot had taken her often to visit the grave of his spiritual friend, Henry David Thoreau. They would go and sit and listen to the birds; sometimes Eliot would play his fife. It was a peaceful, friendly sort of place. The Emersons and Alcotts were there too, and Nathaniel Hawthorne and Daniel Chester French—a whole little community that people made pilgrimages to visit. So now the Commodore was going to be buried there, in Sleepy Hollow; it was odd, but even with all the headstones, she had never thought of anyone actually being buried there.

"—Paula tonight, don't you?" she heard her mother saying. "She should know as soon as possible so she can arrange to get away, and we can set a date for the service."

"Will they want to stay here, do you think?" asked Mr. Paige with a certain lack of enthusiasm.

"I doubt it. She always stays at the Inn when she visits. She says it's more convenient," said Mrs. Paige.

"What about Oliver?" asked Charlotte.

"He might as well stay here. It'll be several days at least before the Prestons come. It seems silly to have him move from here to the Inn. Unless he'd rather."

Charlotte knew he wouldn't.

"What about him? Where is he? Not gone to bed already?" Mr. Paige registered for the first time that he was missing.

"Out walking Amos. He'll be back soon. Charlotte, there's nothing more you can do. Why don't you get ready for bed, darling, you've got shadows under your eyes, and we'll need you in the morning."

"What about school?" Charlotte didn't see how they could go, but she was afraid her parents wouldn't see why they shouldn't. As Oliver had predicted, and she herself had hoped, they had taken over responsibility for what had to be done, and Charlotte and Oliver had became superfluous. It seemed like years since they'd walked away from the high school that afternoon, part of another life. She thought of their class-mates, all of them happily ignorant, unaffected by what had happened—even Andy and Kath—and thought she couldn't face explaining.

"We'll see," said her mother.

As she went up stairs, she heard her father say, "I don't suppose Oliver will know who Sam's lawyer is. I hope to goodness he left a will—"

Lying in the darkness of her room, Charlotte wondered what was going on in Oliver's head; she wished she knew, she wished he would *let* her know. He had come in not long after she started for bed, she recognized his voice downstairs, but it was almost half an hour before he came up. Outside her door she heard his light, familiar step in the hall, and the unmistakable scrabbling of toenails and excited breathing as Amos inhaled his new surroundings. Even though she'd been sure he would come back, she was relieved when he had, and she fell asleep soon after and slept soundly all night.

She woke at the usual time for a school day, as a thin, gray light was filtering into the sky, and lay in a warm cocoon of near-sleep, reluctant to emerge. Friday. Civics, French, alge-bra . . . Her mind cleared instantly. With a flash of cold sick-ness she remembered her French vocabulary test, the algebra homework she hadn't looked at the night before. A split sec-ond behind her French and algebra came the awareness of Oliver, down the hall in Eliot's room. Commodore Shattuck was dead.

Once it came back to her, she couldn't bear to lie still any longer. It was a puzzling word, dead, she reflected as she dressed. She'd taken for granted that she knew what it meant—she'd heard it and used the word herself often enough—now she was doubtful. She struggled to attach it to the Commodore, but he was real and the word abstract, and she had trouble connecting them. She frowned at her image in the bathroom mirror without seeing it and tried to make herself understand that he had gone from the world, not just that she wouldn't see him again. There were lots of people who still existed, whom she had seen and wouldn't see again: people she passed on the street, or sat in movie theaters and at basketball games with, people who moved away. They were still there, taking up space in the world, breathing the air, looking up at a different part of the same sky, eating, talking, brushing their teeth, riding in cars or on buses or bicycles. None of that applied to the Commodore. After Wednesday, January 17th, he ceased being, stopped doing all those things forever, was gone. Furthermore, he'd been gone almost a day before she'd known it.

It was an enormous thing to try to fit her mind around. She wasn't sure how she felt about it and that disturbed her very deeply. She was sure she ought to feel shock and grief and loss instead of this vast bewilderment, this incomprehension.

Her mother was already downstairs, in her bathrobe, awake and organized, although her eyes looked tired. "Good morning, darling, did you sleep?"

Guiltily, Charlotte nodded. She was also hungry and remembered she hadn't taken much interest in her supper the night before, but it didn't seem right to sit down and eat a hearty breakfast. She noticed the cats pacing around the kitchen, edgy, suspicious, unprepared to settle. They hadn't touched the food Mrs. Paige had put down for them.

"Bacon and scrambled eggs, I think," said her mother, coming to her rescue. "No good facing this day on an empty stomach. You can pour the orange juice. Your father's still sleeping. So, I guess, is Oliver."

"No, I'm not." He startled them both. He had come down the front stairs and they hadn't heard him. He stood in the doorway fully dressed, with his jacket on. "I'm going to take Amos out," he said, "just around the house."

Mrs. Paige took two more eggs out of the refrigerator and Charlotte got another glass. When Oliver came back, the bacon was almost done and Charlotte's mouth was watering.

"I left Amos on the porch. He's used to having breakfast and I didn't think to bring any dog chow."

"All we have is cat food," said Charlotte. "Would he eat toast?"

"Not very good for him, but I'm sure he'd like it."

"Do you have your eggs well cooked or runny?" asked Mrs. Paige as Charlotte put two slices of bread in the toaster.

"Hard, please," said Oliver.

It was an absurd conversation, avoiding as it did what they all must be thinking about, and the questions that had to be asked and answered. Oliver took the toast out to Amos with a large bowl of water.

"All right," said Mrs. Paige, "there are a lot of things that need to be discussed and I don't see any point in putting them off." The three of them were sitting around the table; eggs and bacon had disappeared, and Charlotte and Oliver were eating English muffins and Mrs. Paige was drinking coffee. "For a start, there's school." She looked from one to the other of them. Charlotte waited for Oliver to speak first.

After a moment he did. "I would rather not go. There isn't much point now, and I don't want people looking at me sideways all day and asking a lot of stupid questions."

"But they won't know," said Charlotte.

"You don't think so?" he challenged.

"I'm afraid Oliver's probably right." Mrs. Paige set down her cup. "Isn't Jennifer Gilbert in your class? Her father's the funeral director, so she'll know. And anyone who's talked to Dr. Culhane. I'm afraid news like this gets around very fast."

"Uncle Sam's lawyer's son's a senior on the tennis team," added Oliver.

"Well, I haven't done any homework," said Charlotte.

Mrs. Paige nodded. "I think either you both go to school, or you both stay home, so that's settled. Gordon will go see the lawyer and someone at the bank and find out what needs to be done. I'm afraid I've got to spend some time at the building this afternoon—the painters are coming and I can't put them off. But this morning, Oliver, you and I had better make arrangements for the service. That will be with Rever-

73

end Francks at Trinity. Unless you have other ideas, we thought a simple burial and then a memorial service next week."

Oliver, studying his butter-smeared knife, shook his head.

"Good. Then there'll be people who should be called and told." Mrs. Paige watched him as she spoke, a little v hovering between her eyebrows, but Oliver was quite calm. "I expect you know better than anyone which of Sam's friends they are. Perhaps you could decide? You don't have to do the calling."

"What about Paula?" he asked unemotionally.

"I spoke to your mother last night. She's going to call back this morning once she's had a chance to make some arrangements."

"I'll have to get things from the house. I'll need the key."

"Gordon has it. I guess I'd better get dressed." But she hestitated. "Oliver—?"

"What?"

She pulled the cord of her robe tighter, smoothed it. "You'll have to buy some food for Amos. Do you need money?" Whatever her mother had wanted to say, Charlotte didn't think that was it. Mrs. Paige's tone of voice didn't match the words.

"Thank you," he said politely, "but I have enough."

Charlotte was left home, delegated to wait for Paula's phone call and answer any others that might come. The cats had made themselves invisible, the house was silent. She thought of bringing Amos in for company, but he was so big and slobbery she knew she'd lose patience with him very quickly. There was the schoolwork she hadn't done the day before, but when she spread out her books she couldn't keep her mind on the pages.

There was so much to do when somebody died, so many things to think of and see to. Death sounded so final, but it was only final for the person who died. She thought of Oliver, swept up by her mother and taken off to the church to discuss his great-uncle's memorial service. Did they expect him to know what to do? Did he? She wouldn't. She'd never even

74

been to one before. He went without protest, thinking his own thoughts. Since telling her parents the night before, he had withdrawn inside himself and she could not come near him, none of them could.

Had she done the right thing, making him tell? But he had to. She couldn't, she simply couldn't, see any alternative. There were other people he could have told: Dr. Culhane, the lawyer, the police, she supposed, but who better than her parents? They would have had to know anyway. He wanted time to sort things out, but what difference could more time make? He had said it himself, her mother had said it: he was too young to do what he wanted, to take responsibility for his own life; he would not be allowed to. She longed to talk to him, to talk to *some*body about it. She needed reassurance. She thought of Eliot and her eyes swam momentarily and she ached for him. But there was no way of reaching him, even by telephone.

The last time she'd seen him he'd had a beard, a pale curly one, and had just spent the best part of July in the high country of Yosemite, backpacking with a friend of his from graduate school. He talked about going to Alaska, but he had this job lined up in Colorado studying coyotes for the Wildlife Service for a year. He came home at the end of August before it started, because he didn't think he could get away for Christmas. She had known then for a fact what she had begun to suspect soon after he'd left for Montana the first time: that he wouldn't come back to Concord, Massachusetts, to settle again, only to visit. It made her sad, but not heartbroken. She was able by that time to accept without resentment his involvement in something she was not part of. Their lives had diverged.

Eliot's world had expanded; he was bursting with energy and confidence. He talked and talked to everyone who'd listen—about the people he'd met, learned from, gone to school with, the experiences he'd had, the studies he'd done. "But it's the *country*, Charlie!" he exclaimed late one afternoon as they were walking slowly around Great Meadows. The light was golden, thick as honey, the air still. The broad expanse of water on either side of the dike was carpeted with water

75

lily leaves, the seed pods like green shower heads, sticking straight up through them. Nothing moved on the wildlife refuge in the heat except other people strolling the paths. It was hot and peaceful: ripe summer.

"Imagine," said Eliot, "putting your feet where no one else has stepped, hiking where there aren't any trails already hacked out by somebody else. Camping where you can't see another spark of light in the darkness, unless you count the stars."

"I bet you can't," said Charlotte.

"Can't what?"

"Count the stars."

"Smart kid," he said with a grin. "When I think of the expeditions we used to have up Monadnock—single file on the path and try to find room to sit among all the other bodies at the top. It's not the same, I can tell you."

"Isn't it scary?" she asked. "What if something happens to you? What would you do out there?"

"To begin with, you've got to be very careful. Not take stupid risks, carry the right equipment, make sure someone knows approximately where you are and when you're coming out again. I've only actually gone alone once. And actually," he admitted, "it *was* a little scary. But it was a terrific experience. I saw and heard and felt and thought about things I never would have if anyone else had been along. I'm going to do it again, Charlie, but"—he gave her a conspiratorial look—"you don't have to mention it to Mom."

"No," she agreed. They walked in companionable silence and she thought over what he'd said, about being alone. The marsh sang with insects; redwings and wrens called, invisible among the cattails. A man in the path ahead had set up a telescope on a tripod and was peering through it, while another man beside him looked through binoculars. Both wore grubby crew hats against the sun and expressions of great concentration. As Charlotte and Eliot passed them, they could be heard arguing mildly about "pecs" and "semi-pals," which Charlotte assumed were birds of some kind. Eliot gave her a wink. "Hard-core stuff," he said.

"What about me?" she asked him.

"Hmm? Tell you what, Charlie. You get Andy to give you a leave of absence from the farm next summer, and I'll take you camping. Wherever I am. How's that? Then I can show you what I'm talking about."

"Fine," she said, "but that's not what I mean. Do you think I'll ever find something like it, for me?"

He sucked his lower lip thoughtfully. "I don't know, Chuck. I don't see why not if you look hard enough. Of all of us, you know, Max has had the easiest time that way. He knew before he left high school exactly what he wanted to do, and he's doing it, and he's happy as a clam. No doubts, no hesitation, no wrong turns." He sounded mildly envious.

"But you did what you wanted," she pointed out. "And Deb's done what she wanted. No one ever stopped you."

"That's true—we've done what we wanted, but we haven't always known what we wanted to do. There's a difference. I'm not one hundred percent sure now, but this is the closest I've come and it just may be the right thing."

Charlotte sighed. "I can't imagine waking up one morning knowing that all you ever wanted to do was be an architectural engineer. A doctor or a missionary, maybe."

"Or a fireman or president of the United States or filthy rich," said Eliot rubbing his beard. "It's just the sort of person Max is. He knew immediately that he wanted to marry Jean, too. And have a family and assume a mortgage. Lord love him!"

"You know," said Charlotte thoughtfully, "Andy's like that. I hadn't thought of it before, but he is. The only thing Andy wants to be is a farmer. It doesn't matter what his father says against it, there just isn't anything else as far as he's concerned. They used to argue about it, but they don't anymore. Andy says there's no point. If he can't work the Bullard Farm, he'll go somewhere else when he's old enough. Sometimes I get so sick of the farm I can hardly stand it."

"Look!" Eliot nudged her. "A kingfisher." They watched it flash blue and white overhead, making its rattling noise as it flew. "What about Kath, then? Is she still so single-minded about horses?"

"It's not the same. That's more the kind of single-minded-

77

ness you have very intensely for a while, then it burns out and something else takes its place."

"A temporary obsession," said Eliot wisely. "I know all about those. Have the horses turned to ashes now?"

"Not altogether, but she does other things as well. Sports. She's very good," said Charlotte. "Field hockey and basketball and softball. Sometimes we go watch her."

They reached the grassy open space on the far side of the marsh and sat in the slanting sun on an empty bench. It was so good to have Eliot there beside her; she remembered the feeling vividly. She had been so afraid that things between them would change when he went away, and they had changed, but she needn't have been afraid. With Eliot, as more recently with Deb, their age difference seemed to matter less and less. In some non-chronological way she was catching up to them.

He had asked about Oliver then. If Oliver knew what he wanted to do, and Charlotte had said, "I'm not sure. He knows what he doesn't want to do—to live with either of his parents again. He does what will keep that from happening."

And Eliot had said, "That's one way of determining your life."

Oliver had done everything he possibly could to achieve his end: he settled down in Concord, made himself useful and agreeable to his great-uncle, caused no trouble in school—on the contrary, he set himself to study hard and do well. He, like Charlotte, had spent most of the last three summers working on Andy's farm, not because he passionately wanted to grow and sell vegetables as Andy did, but because if he were obviously engaged in a productive occupation, he was unlikely to have to spend the long vacation in Washington with his mother and stepfather.

There was nothing he could do about his great-uncle Sam's death; in an instant that had wiped out all his most determined efforts.

Chapter Ten

MIDMORNING THE TELEPHONE BEGAN TO RING. CHARLOTTE'S mother and Oliver had been right: it didn't take long for the news to leak out into the town. During his life in Concord, Commodore Shattuck had accumulated a great many friends and acquaintances, of whom, Charlotte realized, she had been aware of relatively few. She didn't know what to say to the callers; she felt uncomfortable and inadequate, and her heart sank each time the phone rang. It was a relief to answer and hear Deb's level, familiar voice among the others.

"Charlotte? Mother's not there, I suppose. I really am so sorry. It was a shock."

"How did you find out?"

"Jackie Peterson told me when he brought the mail. How are you holding up?"

"Not very well," confessed Charlotte. "There've been seven phone calls already this morning, mostly from people I don't know. I don't know what to say. I wish someone else were here to do this."

"Just thank them for calling, that's all you can do," advised her sister practically. "And write their names down. What about Oliver? How's he doing?"

"He seems very calm, but I—"

"Charlotte—sorry. I've got to go. There're customers waiting. Ask Mother to give me a call—best after work. Okay? Just hang in there, you'll be all right."

Charlotte was not altogether convinced. Just after eleven, Oliver's mother called.

"Hello, Charlotte? Is your mother there? No? I was afraid I'd miss her. Would you give her a message, please? I've got everything arranged here for the twenty-third. Eric and I will fly up late Monday afternoon—we have reservations at the Inn for two nights. We'll just have to take care of as much as we can in that time—we can't be away any longer, either one of us. What's that? He's where? Excuse me a minute, Charlotte—"

Charlotte waited while Paula Preston held a muffled conversation with someone else at her end of the telephone. In a minute she was back again. "Where was I?"

"Getting to Boston on Monday," said Charlotte.

"Yes, thanks. We'll get ourselves to Concord, tell Kit not to worry about that."

"All right," said Charlotte. "She—"

"I'm so sorry your parents are having to cope with everything. I've been afraid for some time this would happen—of course it was bound to. I hope Oliver isn't being difficult. He isn't, is he?"

"Oh no, he hasn't—"

"Good. I'm relieved to hear it. Would you tell your mother I'll be in after seven tonight. I'll call again. I'm late for a meeting right this minute. Tell her how grateful I am, will you? Thank you, Charlotte."

Charlotte was left with a pad full of notes and a helpless, unhappy feeling. There was such a jungle of details springing up to obscure the one important thing: Commodore Shattuck's death. Life didn't stop for everyone because it stopped for one person, she didn't expect that. But she hadn't expected it to speed up, either. It distressed her.

When Mrs. Paige and Oliver came home for lunch, Charlotte was more than happy to let her mother deal with the phone instead. Oliver wouldn't do it. "I don't want to listen to people tell me how sorry they are," he stated flatly. "I haven't got anything to say."

Mrs. Paige gave him an odd look, but said nothing until he went upstairs. "I wish I knew what to do about him. He's so self-contained and unemotional. I'd find him much easier to understand if he'd just let go, even a little. He hardly said a word while we were with Tim Francks, I wasn't even sure he was listening."

"If he doesn't want you to see what he's thinking he doesn't show you," said Charlotte. "He's always been like that."

"But darling, it isn't as if he doesn't know us. And we're very sympathetic. Frankly, he worries me." She sighed. "Still. We'd better have lunch and I'll do some phoning myself before I go meet the painters. Paula said she'd call back when?"

"Was it awful?" asked Charlotte as she and Oliver sat alone over the remains of a hasty lunch.

"Was what awful?" asked Oliver absently, folding a piece of waxed paper into smaller and smaller squares.

"Talking to the minister. Arranging things."

"No, it wasn't awful. It just seemed pointless. I can't see what it's all for—it won't make any difference to Uncle Sam who says what and which hymns are sung. I wanted to ask why we were bothering."

"I hope you didn't," said Charlotte. "That would really have upset Mother."

His eyes shifted to her. "What did she say?"

"I mean, it isn't what people usually ask, is it?" she said to cover her embarrassment; she knew he'd guessed they'd been talking about him.

"Isn't it?"

"I wouldn't think so. When someone dies there's always a funeral."

"This isn't a funeral, it's a memorial service. They're different," he said cooly. "Uncle Sam will have been buried by then."

Charlotte thought it was time to change the subject. "Your mother called. She's coming on Monday, so's your stepfather. They're staying at the Inn."

Oliver absorbed the news without enthusiasm. "Did she ask about me?"

"Of course," said Charlotte a little too vigorously.

"I can imagine. Look, can we talk about something else?"

81

He sat up in his chair, straightening his shoulders.

"Sure. What?"

"Dinner, for instance."

"Dinner? You mean *our* dinner? Tonight?"

"That's right. We can plan it, go and shop for it, then cook it."

"But—"

"I have to buy Amos's food anyway," he pointed out.

"Well, yes," said Charlotte, at a loss. "But dinner. I don't know a lot about cooking, Oliver."

"That doesn't matter. I do."

"What about money?"

"I have plenty. I have most of Uncle Sam's Social Security. Don't look at me that way, he won't need it," he added with brutal logic.

Bemused, Charlotte gave in. There wasn't much else she could do except refuse to join him, but she couldn't think of a good reason for that. At least it would give them something to fill up the afternoon with, and her mother could hardly object.

They pulled out a variety of Mrs. Paige's cookbooks and settled to the task of planning a menu. Charlotte approached it tentatively, looking for things that sounded simplest from the least complicated cookbooks. Oliver plunged into the more exotic, intricate recipes.

"What does it mean, sauté?"

"Brown gently in butter."

"That doesn't sound hard. Here, what about this one?" she said, passing him a book.

He scanned the page and shook his head. "Fish is no good. I only buy it in Bedford—the stuff they sell in the supermarkets is miserable. Uncle Sam loved a nice piece of bluefish, and scallops in garlic butter when we felt extravagant. But they did things to his digestion."

"When did you learn to cook?" she asked curiously.

"I've been doing it for a while." He was noncommittal. "It's not so hard once you understand the basics."

"When we came to dinner last time—in November—who

cooked that meal? You or the Commodore?"

"We both did. He had his specialities and I had mine." He returned to his perusal of *The Flavour of Concord*, one of Mrs. Paige's most trusted sources of inspiration. She had contributed some of her own recipes to it. Charlotte gazed at him speculatively for several minutes.

They finally agreed on something called Tarragon Chicken Trieste. It sounded difficult to Charlotte, but Oliver was confident. They drew up a shopping list. "Have you got any wine?" he asked. "It takes a cup of white wine, and we can't buy it ourselves."

"There's usually a carafe in the fridge. Does it matter what kind? Wait a minute, let me—is that the doorbell?"

They looked at each other. Unmistakably the doorbell rang again. From the sunporch Amos started barking, a reverberant bass that made Charlotte jump.

"Let's pretend we didn't hear it. We aren't here," said Oliver. "Whoever it is doesn't know we're home."

Charlotte hesitated. "What if it's important? We can't just ignore it."

"Why not? In another five minutes we'd have gone to the store."

"But we haven't yet. You stay here and I'll go."

He scowled at her, but stopped arguing.

It was Kath Schuyler on the front doorstep, looking very ill at ease. "I'm glad it's you," she said in obvious relief. She was nervous of Charlotte's parents.

"Come in, so I can close the door," said Charlotte, as Kath hovered outside. "Isn't there basketball practice this afternoon?"

"I cut it. You know what they're saying all over school?"

"I can guess."

"But it isn't true, is it? I mean, you and Oliver, when you didn't show up—I didn't want to call the Commodore's house in case—I came here instead." Kath was plainly agitated. "What's happening?"

"What are they saying?"

"All kinds of stupid things about the Commodore. That

83

he had a heart attack. That he's in Emerson Hospital. That he was taken to Boston with a stroke. Even that he's—he's dead."

Charlotte sucked in a breath. "He is."

Kath just stared at her. Charlotte had the peculiar sense of having been through this identical scene before, only she had had Kath's part the last time. She was sorry she'd been so blunt, but it was the truth and how could she have led into it gently?

"Where's Oliver?" asked Kath in a whisper.

"He's here. He stayed with us last night. He's in the kitchen if you want to see him."

"Well." Kath looked appalled. "I'm not sure. Does he—is he—?"

"You might as well," said Charlotte.

Oliver was taking stock of the refrigerator. He turned to Charlotte, saw Kath, and said, "I can't find any sour cream. You'd better put it on the list."

It was obvious that Kath didn't know what to say. She stood awkward and tongue-tied just inside the kitchen door, looking miserably at him, and Charlotte felt a sudden, genuine sympathy for her. "Kath came to see you," she said. "She cut basketball."

"Why?" said Oliver, deliberately unhelpful. "Where are your herbs?"

"In the drawer by the sink," said Charlotte. "Oliver—"

"When you weren't at school, I thought—well, I—something must be wrong. I didn't know." Kath sounded wretched.

"There are a lot of stories going around school," Charlotte said.

"There always are." With his back to them, Oliver rooted among the herbs and spices.

In junior high there had been stories about Commodore Shattuck and his house: that he was a madman or a miser, that his house was decorated like the inside of a ship or hadn't been cleaned in years. And then stories about his great-nephew: that he had fits, was unbalanced, had had a nervous breakdown. None of them was true. The Commodore's house was quite ordinary inside, and though he was a character, it was of the nicest, least sinister, kind. Oliver was the son of divorced parents who didn't know what to do with him. He was unhappy, rather than unbalanced.

"Has anyone got the right story this time?" he asked.

"Yes," said Charlotte.

"Well, that makes a change, doesn't it," he said evenly, his face opaque.

"Oh," said Kath. "It's so awful. I'm sorry. Is there—can I do anything?"

"No thank you," said Oliver politely. "There isn't anything anyone can do. It's irrevocable."

Charlotte glared at him, her mouth compressed in the way that warned her family she was losing her temper, but he ignored her.

Kath looked as if she wished she could vanish, but she was rooted to the spot. She was trying so painfully hard it made Charlotte's stomach wrench. "What will happen now?" she asked in a small voice. "What will you do?"

"I won't have to do anything—it'll be done for me. Whether I like it or not. Charlotte, I think we'd better do the shopping before it gets any later."

She could think of only one way to help Kath. "I've got to get my jacket," she said brusquely and took Kath's arm and pulled her into the front hall. Kath offered no resistance. "You've got to understand," said Charlotte in an undertone, "it was so sudden. The Commodore was all right last Sunday. They were coming to supper tonight. Nobody expected it. And you know how Oliver is." She was making excuses; they sounded feeble, but Kath nodded mutely.

"When did you find out?"

"Yesterday. Look, Kath, he probably won't be so hard to talk to in a day or so."

"Should I tell anyone?"

"It's hardly a secret," said Charlotte tartly. "You might as well. It's better than having people make things up."

"It's just—I can't believe it. I can't—I never thought . . ." Her voice trailed away and she stood staring at the doorknob.

"I know. It's hard." Charlotte was eager for her to leave.

The combination of Kath's wretchedness and Oliver's impenetrability oppressed her dreadfully; she didn't think she could stand much more of it. "I'll talk to you soon, okay? I'll let you know what's going on."

"Call tomorrow. Promise?" said Kath urgently.

"I promise." Charlotte practically pushed her out the door, then closed it firmly and leaned against it.

"Is she gone?" Oliver emerged in the shadows at the end of the hall.

"You could have been nicer to her," Charlotte said sharply.

"Nicer? What was I supposed to do? Sob on her shoulder? Smile bravely through my tears? I'm sorry, Charlotte, I don't do that kind of thing."

Her mouth tightened ominously.

"Don't let's argue about it. Please."

She couldn't see his face clearly in the dim light, but there was a note of desperation in his voice that brought her up short, made her swallow what she'd been about to say. "Oliver—"

"Just put on your coat and let's go. Let's get out of here now, before anything else happens."

They took the Commodore's car, although Charlotte didn't want to. It didn't seem right to use it, but Oliver said that was nonsense. If they didn't, who would? And how else would they get the groceries back? She gave in without much struggle; she suddenly felt tired and dismal. If only Kath hadn't burst in and behaved so awkwardly, thought Charlotte irritably. All she had accomplished was to upset things.

The afternoon was gray to match her mood. A bitter little wind rattled the trees; there was a bite to it that promised snow before long. If life hadn't been turned upside down, Charlotte reflected, they would be looking forward to good tobogganing the next day.

The supermarket was full of flat, gritty light and what Eliot called "condensed soup music," gluey and bland. Oliver took a cart and pushed it slowly up and down the aisles. He knew where everything was, but it was unfamiliar to Charlotte; her mother used the Stop & Shop on the other side of town. But the ordinariness of it—the smeared floors, the shelves of breakfast cereals and soft drinks, the other people, looking dazed or intent or distracted, even the dreary music, had a calming effect on her. And Oliver had himself well in hand again. He had patched the crack that had earlier threatened his composure.

Together they weighed out fresh mushrooms, found the scallions, picked over the plastic-wrapped chicken breasts until Oliver found enough that met with his approval. "They're more expensive boned, but it's worth it," he explained knowledgeably. "That broccoli looks nice. And we can have baked potatoes."

"I hope you know what to do with it," said Charlotte, eyeing the green vegetable with doubt.

They picked out crackers and cheese, potato chips and clam dip—Charlotte's idea—six cans of dog food, and a ten-pound bag of dog chow. "How much does he eat, anyway?" asked Charlotte as Oliver loaded these into the cart.

"He's a big dog," said Oliver.

She found cooking with Oliver an experience. He followed a recipe precisely, step by careful step. He did not believe in shortcuts, substitutions, or embellishments. He measured ingredients exactly. "If that's the way it's written, that's the way it should be done. Otherwise it won't come out right." Charlotte wasn't totally convinced. When her mother cooked she had several different cookbooks lying open on the counters and took bits from all or none of them, depending on how she felt and what was in the refrigerator.

But what Oliver said made sense, she had to admit. *Some-one* had worked out and tested each recipe so it would succeed, before printing it in a cookbook. Anyway, she hadn't the experience to challenge him. She never would have undertaken such a meal on her own. She could do survival food: grilled cheese sandwiches, BLTs, even hamburgers, and, if she put her mind to it, macaroni and cheese—though the last time, she had done everything right up to the end and forgotten to turn on the oven. Mrs. Paige pushed gently now and then, but didn't nag at her to learn, the way other mothers

87

did. Deb was actually more severe, but now that she wasn't living at home, she seldom mentioned it. Charlotte didn't really know whether Deb herself was a good cook or not. The kinds of things she normally produced made it hard to tell: they were healthy, often unidentifiable, and strange.

By the time Mrs. Paige found them, they had the chicken ready to cook, the mushrooms browned, the broccoli cut up, and the potatoes scrubbed and in the oven.

"Do I live here?" she asked quizzically.

Charlotte had been braced for some kind of remark, but Oliver said, "I hope you don't mind. We thought since we had time, we'd fix dinner".

"Mind? I should say not. It smells wonderful, whatever it is."

"We haven't cooked it yet," said Charlotte shortly.

"It must be the intent I smell then," Mrs. Paige replied. "I wonder when your father will get home, and what kind of day he's had. I don't suppose you've heard from him. Where did you get mushrooms?"

"We went out, shopping," said Charlotte. "We had to buy dog food." She hoped her mother wouldn't ask where the money had come from, suspecting she would not approve.

"Oh, of course. Amos. I'm glad you didn't stay in all day. I'll go change my clothes."

"Actually," said Oliver to Charlotte, "there isn't a lot more we can do until we know when we're going to eat. Timing things to come out right is the trickiest part. We can do the cheese and dip, though."

"Do?"

"Arrange them on plates."

It was as if they were getting ready for a party—the dinner Oliver and his great-uncle were supposed to be coming for that evening, not an ordinary family meal. She almost expected him to suggest straightening and vacuuming the living room. He didn't. Instead he asked, "Would your parents mind if we had a fire? I saw wood on the sunporch."

"No, I don't suppose so." Eliot had taken responsibility for fireplace fires. He taught Charlotte how to build them efficiently, but since he'd gone, she didn't do it very often. He

88

used to sit on the floor, as close as he could get to the flames without singeing, and soak up the heat, an expression of bliss on his face and a cat on his lap.

Charlotte closed the curtains against the cold darkness, and Oliver knelt on the hearth working on the fire. He had trouble getting the wood to catch—he was concentrating very hard, frowning. She almost said, "Here, let me." She almost interrupted to show him how to make one of Eliot's newspaper fans, but held herself back and pretended not to notice that he was struggling.

They were all in the living room, around Oliver's fire, nudging cheese and crackers and now and then a potato chip, when Mr. Paige came home. The cats were secured in the kitchen, and even Amos was there, sprawled untidily on the rug, head flat, gazing with devotion at the cheese plate. "What a scene of domestic tranquility," remarked Mr. Paige. "It's snowing again." He made drinks for himself and Mrs. Paige. "That wouldn't by any chance be clam dip, would it?"

No one mentioned Commodore Shattuck, or discussed what had occupied them each most of the day. It was as if they had sworn a temporary pact. They watched the Boston news on television, as the Paiges did every evening—the usual fires, political messes, basketball and hockey scores, six to eight inches of snow. At quarter to seven, Oliver went out to the kitchen to finish cooking the chicken. Charlotte scooped up a last chipful of dip and went after him.

"It's all right," he said. "There's not much to do."

"It's my dinner too, you know."

Except for Oliver's directions, they worked silently. When everything was nearly ready, he sent her to announce it while he dished up. She noticed that her father had refilled his glass and that Amos was sitting next to him, resting his hairy chin on a couch cushion, eyes glued to the piece of cheese Mr. Paige held. The newscasters had changed; someone was talking about the hostages in Tehran. "Was he on?" asked Charlotte suddenly. "Oliver's stepfather?"

Mrs. Paige nodded. "Gordon, that dog's going to have your cheese in a minute, if you aren't careful."

"We'll split it, shall we?" said Mr. Paige equably as he

89

took a bite and gave the rest to Amos. Still sitting, Amos inched closer.

"Dad," said Charlotte reprovingly.

"You don't have to tell Oliver. It's between Amos and me. Isn't it?" Amos gave his tail a thump at the sound of his name and looked hopeful. "Is Eric Preston coming?" he inquired.

"That's what Paula told Charlotte this morning. They'll both be here Monday evening."

"I'd rather like to meet him." Mr. Paige grinned. "I hope Deb isn't feeling political."

"Oh, lord," said Mrs. Paige. "You'll have to have a talk with her before. If only she didn't go at people that way."

"Dinner's ready," Charlotte said.

It was a success although the broccoli was overdone and slightly mushy. Oliver pointed it out immediately—no one else would have. But the before-dinner mood had changed somehow. There was a tension underneath the casual-seeming conversation; they tried to keep up the pretense, but there was an awareness that they were avoiding the matter that was uppermost in all of their thoughts. Once again, Charlotte found it difficult to eat; her stomach was tight and unwilling.

"Don't you like it?" asked Oliver, looking at her plate as he gave Mr. Paige a second piece of chicken.

"Things often don't taste as good to the cook," said Mrs. Paige, coming to her rescue. "I don't know why, but making a meal frequently takes the edge off my appetite. On the other hand, *not* having to cook makes me twice as hungry. Is there another little piece, Oliver? That's fine."

Paula called again while they were having dessert. Charlotte watched her mother's ice cream melt while she was on the phone in the den. Her father and Oliver talked about dogs. "I had one when I was in high school—a wire-haired fox terrier, grand little dog. Bitsey. I have a picture of him somewhere. What do you think's in that dog of yours anyway, Oliver?"

"Dr. Russell says wolfhound, maybe poodle. Both his parents were probably mongrels."

"He's got personality," pronounced Mr. Paige. "And you've got him well-trained."

"He's a smart dog. Aren't you, Amos?" Amos had taken up a position just outside the dining room, lying with his nose between his paws, where he could keep track of everything that went on. When Oliver spoke to him, he raised his improbable head. "No, stay," said Oliver firmly. Amos subsided.

"Wonder what he'll make of city life," said Mr. Paige.

Charlotte saw Oliver stiffen, but he continued eating his ice cream with scarcely a hesitation. "I don't know," he said after a minute.

Chapter Eleven

MOST DAYS CHARLOTTE READ THE FUNNIES IN THE DAILY newspaper. Her mother read the news sections and the editorials, her father read sports and the editorials, and they both read the obituaries. Their interest in deaths seemed to Charlotte rather ghoulish. Her mother said it was something that came with age. Her father said it was his business to know who died; a large part of the museum's income was from bequests. And when he was in one of his increasingly frequent ill-humors over his Board of Directors or Trustees, he was heard to remark that many people only bothered to *be* Trustees in the first place because it looked good in their obituaries. "Mrs. Langhorne Peak-Freen, pillar of the community, champion of the arts, Trustee of the Pierce-Courtland Museum. Never mind that she did none of the actual work. She lent us her illustrious name, after all!"

"Your father's ranting again," Mrs. Paige would say dryly.

Saturday morning Charlotte found the *Globe* open to the obituary section on the dining room table. There was the Commodore's name in black, hard print: Samuel Prescott Shattuck, of Concord. There was quite a long notice and a photograph of a rather stout man in a naval uniform who bore a distinct resemblance to the weathered, white-haired little man Charlotte had known. The caption said it had been taken in 1967—she was two that year. It wasn't the uniform that made him look not-quite familiar, she'd seen him in it every Patriot's, Memorial, and Veteran's Day, even before she'd known him personally. She stared at the picture for a long time, chewing her lip thoughtfully.

"Who wrote this?" she asked her father, who was pulling himself together and drinking a second cup of coffee. He was going, with utmost reluctance, to spend Saturday morning at the museum in order to catch up on the things he had neglected the day before. It meant that he would miss his weekly luncheon in Boston, and he was not pleased.

"What? Oh. Arthur Hodgson. Sam's lawyer suggested him. I hadn't known they were friends."

"Have you heard of him?"

He looked at her over the rim of his cup. "You haven't?"

She shook her head. "Who is he?"

"Ask your mother. I've got to shave."

"Who's Arthur Hodgson?" Charlotte asked her mother. Mrs. Paige was in the den, shuffling piles of paper on her desk.

"A famous naval historian, darling. There's a shelf of his books upstairs in Max's old room."

"Are they Max's?"

"No, your grandfather DeWolf's. And the later ones are mine. Have a look at them sometime, he writes very well. He did a nice obituary for Sam, don't you think?"

"I guess. It's like reading about someone I didn't know. He never talked about half the things he did. I didn't know any of that stuff about the Saint Lawrence Seaway, or that he taught at a prep school for nine years."

"He lived most of his life before you were born," her mother pointed out. "It's like layers of paint on an old building—the early ones keep getting covered. You don't see them. A lot of people will miss Sam, I suspect. Has your father gone yet?"

"He's upstairs, shaving."

"I've got to talk to him about the house. Max and Jean are coming out tomorrow and Jean's offered to help with it."

"What do you mean, help?"

"It has to be closed temporarily, until the Prestons decide what's to be done with it. The refrigerator has to be cleaned out, the heat and electricity checked, the phone turned off, the trash and garbage dumped"—she was checking a list as she spoke—"and Oliver will have to pack his clothes. The Prestons won't have time to do all that."

Charlotte felt cold. Her mother's list depressed her terribly with its inescapable finality.

"It has to be done. I'm not looking forward to it, either, Charlotte, but it's better to get it over with."

"This morning—I thought I'd go out to the farm." She avoided her mother's eyes. "Andy has the day off. We were all going to do something together."

"Yes, all right. But you'll have to be home in time for the interment this afternoon. It's at one-thirty."

It was too much; Charlotte couldn't think about it. She nodded and turned to flee.

"And tell Oliver—"

"I don't know where he is." She stopped in the doorway.

"He's going with you, isn't he?"

"I hadn't—no, I don't think so. I don't think he particularly wants to see anyone right now."

Mrs. Paige looked up from her papers; her expression was a mixture of concern and exasperation. "But he can't shut himself off that way, Charlotte."

"He's done it before," she replied. "That's the way he is. Kath came yesterday after school and it was pretty awful. She didn't know what to say to him and he didn't help much."

"Poor Kath," said Mrs. Paige with sympathy. "It must have taken courage for her to come."

"But she was so awkward about it, Mom. She didn't have the sense to leave him alone when she saw what kind of mood he was in. She ought to know Oliver better by this time."

"Darling, Oliver is not an easy person to know. He's your friend, but even you have to admit that."

Charlotte stared through a window. Outside the sun was bright, blinding on the new snow and the wind was busy rearranging the drifts. The light caught streaks of dirt on the glass.

"I don't envy Paula," Mrs. Paige went on. "She's going to have her hands full with him, I think. I often wondered how on earth he and Sam managed to get along together."

94

"They got along together very well," asserted Charlotte. "You know they did. They were good company for each other—Oliver did all kinds of things for the Commodore. He ran errands and shoveled snow and did a lot of the cooking. And he's done well at school, and worked hard at the farm. Everything's been fine."

"Yes, I know. But it can't have been easy for Sam to suddenly find himself responsible for a teenaged boy. He was nearly eighty when Oliver came, darling, and Oliver didn't have a very promising history to recommend him."

"That wasn't Oliver's fault—a lot of it wasn't. What about his parents? They started sending him away to school when he was only eight," protested Charlotte hotly. "I think that was a lousy thing to do."

"*They* didn't, Charlotte, Paula did. Oliver's father has taken virtually no responsibility for him in years. And maybe sending him away was the best thing she could do for him at that time. You don't know the situation."

"You mean you think it was right?" Charlotte was unbelieving.

"No, love, it's not that simple. One side isn't right and the other wrong—it doesn't work that way. Can you possibly imagine what it would be like to find yourself alone with an eight-year-old child and no idea of what you were going to do with your life and how you were going to cope?"

"I'd take care of my eight-year-old child," declared Charlotte. "You would have too, I bet."

Mrs. Paige looked at her thoughtfully. "I hope you and Oliver both will give Paula a chance, darling. She's not a bad person, honestly she's not. She's had a hard time, too. And I'll tell you something else, she's a little scared of Oliver. Because of everything that's happened and because she doesn't know him very well."

"How could she? She hasn't spent much time with him."

"No, but she's going to. That's the way it is for both of them, at least until Oliver's independent."

"Unless she sends him away again," said Charlotte. "If she sent him to Middlesex Academy he wouldn't have to leave Concord," she added hopefully.

95

But Mrs. Paige shook her head. "She isn't going to send him away, not this time. The circumstances are quite different. They'll both have to adjust—Paula knows that, and she's willing to work at it. She wants to, she's told me. I hope Oliver will have the good sense to understand it too, because there isn't any choice. If you can help him, darling, try your best. I think he's been very lucky to have landed here in Concord and to have found such good friends, and I hope he knows that."

"He's been a good friend to me, too, don't forget," said Charlotte.

"Of course he has," agreed her mother, a little too positively. "Now, I suggest you catch your father before he leaves for the museum and ask him to drop you at the farm on his way."

"I thought you wanted to talk to him."

"It can wait until this afternoon. I have plenty to do as it is. Go on, quick. I think I hear him in the hall."

Mr. Paige took Charlotte as far as the Antiquarian Museum on Lexington Road, about a mile from the farm. "Are you sure this is all right?" he asked hopefully, with a glance at his dashboard clock. "I can take you the whole way, Charlie; it's only a small detour."

"No, it's fine. The walk will be good."

"How'll you get home?"

"Andy or Skip. Someone can drive me." She shut the car door and her father drove off, lifting his hand in farewell. She shivered involuntarily; the wind struck cold against her after the warm shelter of the car. For a moment she hesitated, there at the crossroad, wondering why she had come and if she should go on. Without thinking much about it, she had chosen the farm as the place to go to get away from her own house; she felt she had to go somewhere. When she'd felt that before there had been a choice: the farm, or the Commodore's house.

But staring down the road, she was suddenly not sure. What would she find at the farm? What did she want to find? Pat would probably be there, and the Tinies—the three smallest

Schuyler children: Cindy, Carl, and six-year-old Paddy; their presence would be distracting and reassuring. Skip and George would probably be out. Kath—she wasn't at all sure she wanted to see Kath after yesterday. She'd only promised to call, that would be easier than seeing Kath face to face. And there was Andy. She wondered how he was taking this. Intuitively she knew the answer: hard.

Andy had a bad time coping with illness and injury—other people's or his own. It tied him in knots, made him and everyone else feel doubly miserable because he couldn't handle it. Last October, when Charlotte had gone to the hospital with appendicitis, it had been Oliver who'd visited her while she was there, coming every afternoon after school with some silly little gift: a book of cartoons, a box of crayons, a miniature puzzle, a small stuffed pig. The pig—Wilbur—sat on her pillow at home. Even Kath came to see her when she was out of the hospital, recuperating. Of Andy there had been no sign. His apparent lack of concern surprised Charlotte. She was hurt by it. When she asked Kath about him, his sister explained brusquely that he was worse than useless under such circumstances. It wasn't that he didn't care—he plagued Kath and Oliver with questions about her. But he was afraid, and mortified because of it.

She remembered how, the first summer at the farm, they had been down in one of the overgrown fields together, and Andy had stepped on a half-buried, rusty piece of machinery—a plow blade or a cultivator. It had sliced right through his sneaker deep into his foot. If Charlotte hadn't become aware of the sudden stillness and gone to find him, sitting in the grass, looking white as chalk and watching himself bleed, he would have sat there until he bled to death. Poor old Andy.

But it was chilly and there was no point standing around indecisively, so she set out toward the farm. On her right lay the Town Forest. On the left were houses: small, unprepossessing, blue, pink, and yellow ones mostly. Some had shutters with little minutemen cut out of them, wooden lean-tos over the shrubs in their front yards to keep the snow off, Christmas wreaths still on their front doors, neatly shoveled walks and driveways. Isolated among them were the remnants of a few old farms, their fields eaten away by developments, their barns shabby and derelict, big maples or oaks or the broad stumps of elms in front of the houses, testifying to their age.

Between two of the pastel newcomers, a gang of kids was building a snow fort. The air was full of shouting and laughter, snowballs and argument. Charlotte watched them for a few minutes enviously before trudging on. They were immersed in the kind of boisterous activity that she and Andy, Oliver and Kath had engaged in many times together. It was what they should have been doing that very day, in fact, in the sun and the snow. She wondered gloomily if they ever would again, in the same thoughtless, frivolous way.

The french doors into the Schuylers' living room were unlocked as usual. Charlotte let herself in after wiping her feet, stuffed her hat, scarf, and mittens carefully into one of her parka sleeves so they wouldn't get lost among all the others scattered about, and laid the parka on top of a heap of jackets and coats on one of the chairs. The room was cold, deserted, and dim; heavy opaque sheets of plastic had been taped over the glass doors to weatherproof them, and the curtains were pulled across the windows. During the winter the Schuylers used the room as an enormous coat closet, and retreated to the kitchen, pantry, and dining room to live, all on top of one another until warm weather came again. They sacrificed privacy for warmth. There was no way, George Schuyler said, that he could afford to heat the whole house as well as pay taxes on it. Somehow the eight Schuylers, Skip Bullard, and the dog Alice managed to get through the winter without murdering one another.

Charlotte had gotten used to the noise and confusion of their daily existence; she actually enjoyed it in moderate doses, but she was quite sure she couldn't live in the middle of it all the time. It was all in what you were used to, she supposed. Her own house, with its space and quiet, seemed to make Kath and Andy uneasy.

The twins, Cindy and Carl, were in the kitchen. Cindy was greasing an oblong pan, while Carl stirred something gooey and white in a double boiler on the stove, his tongue stuck out in concentration.

"Where is everyone?" asked Charlotte.

"Around," said Carl, unwilling to be distracted.

Cindy, full of information as usual, gave her a more satisfactory answer. "Kath and Paddy are down bird-feeding, Andy's splitting wood, don't know about Dan, Ma's sorting stuff in there"—she nodded toward the dining room—"Pa and Skip're at work. You ever make Rice Krispies bars, Charlie?"

"With marshmallows?" Charlotte nodded enthusiastically.

"Okay, they're melted," announced Carl.

"Three minutes," Cindy read off the cereal box. "Keep stirring." She fixed her eyes on the kitchen clock.

Charlotte left them to their project, hoping she'd be around when the marshmallow cooled. The long table in the dining room was littered with piles and bags and boxes: Pat's craft supplies. She filled the little cracks in her days all year round by making cards and gift tags and Christmas ornaments: little knitted mice, crocheted snowflakes, cork and pipe-cleaner reindeer, walnut shell turtles, felt birds, construction paper Santa Clauses. She sold them at church fairs or gave them as presents or kept them for her own family. She was extremely ingenious and could turn the most unpromising scraps and discards into decorations. People were always giving her bagfuls of things they had no use for, but couldn't bring themselves to throw away: scraps of cloth, egg cartons, used greeting cards, leftover yarn, empty spools. At that moment, however, she wasn't sorting, she was bent over, her elbows against the table in the middle of the chaos, reading a letter. "Did you remember to run hot water in the marshmallow pot?" she asked without looking up.

"They aren't through yet," said Charlotte.

Pat jerked her head around. "Charlotte, I'm sorry! I thought you were Cindy." She straightened her back with a slight wince and blew at the fringe of tan hair on her forehead; her single braid was starting to unravel. She was wearing baggy, paint-spotted jeans and an old brown pullover, thin at the elbows. "You caught me. I'm supposed to be organizing all this, but I got hung up rereading Christmas cards." She surveyed the table critically. "It's a mess, isn't it."

Tactfully, Charlotte kept silent and Pat grinned at her. "We'll never be able to eat meals here again at this rate. Or we'll have to get a new dining room table. Like the Mad Hatter—'No room, no room!' George is going to be very depressed if he comes home and I haven't cleaned it up."

"Maybe I could help," offered Charlotte. Pat's messes intrigued her. "I don't mind."

"It hardly seems fair, but if you aren't in a hurry maybe you could just put things together—all the yarn in that bag, for instance. That would be wonderful."

"What are these?" asked Charlotte after a while. She held up a little crocheted star with two eyes and a hole in the middle.

"That's a button monster. See? It buttons on your shirt like that." Pat buttoned him on her. "Neat, isn't he? Would Hilary like him? Take her one, why don't you."

"Thanks. She'll be out tomorrow. Max and Jean are coming to help with the Commodore's house."

Pat's expression softened. "Oh, Charlie, I'm sorry. I'm so sorry about Sam. He was such a wonderful person and a dear friend. We'll miss him terribly."

Charlotte's eyes stung, and she didn't trust her voice for a moment.

"If there's anything at all I can do—or any of us—you'll say, won't you? I ought to have called your mother, but I was afraid she'd be terribly busy. I didn't know . . ." Pat sounded apologetic. She looked down at her hands, watching them straighten stacks of cards. There was an awkward little pause. "What about the service? When's that?"

"Tuesday afternoon at Trinity. People will come to our house afterward." The details were concrete; it was easier to talk about them than feelings. "Mother thought that would be the best thing."

"I could make something to bring," Pat offered immediately. "You know, brownies or banana bread, so long as it isn't too fancy. Tell your mother I'll do that." She sounded distinctly relieved. "Kath said Oliver's with you. What about his family?"

"His mother and stepfather are coming Monday—I don't know about his father. Mother said we should leave that to Paula—to Mrs. Preston."

"Mrs. Preston?"

"Oliver's mother. Paula."

"Yes, of course," said Pat. "It's stupid of me—I always forget. I don't know why."

"She doesn't come very often, and she doesn't stay long. She can't leave her job, she says."

"Yes." Pat made a wry face. "I bet *her* dining room table doesn't look like this."

Charlotte glanced quickly at her; there was a funny little edge in Pat's voice that she didn't recognize. "I bet she doesn't know how to make button monsters."

Pat gave an explosive laugh. "Now that's a bet I wouldn't touch with a barge pole! You don't suppose the National Endowment for the Arts would give me a grant to make them, do you, Charlie? Regional folk art? No. Oh, well." She grabbed a double handful of felt scraps and stuffed them any way into a plastic bag. "I'm sick of the sight of this junk. Why don't you go find Andy? He'd be glad to see you." She began to sweep things together and bundle them indiscriminately into shoe boxes and cartons. "Charlie—"

Charlotte turned back to her. "What?"

"You know Andy. He's quite upset about this; you should be prepared. He can't help it, he doesn't hide things well."

And Oliver hides them too well, thought Charlotte. There ought to be an in-between.

The twins were no longer in the kitchen; they had cleared out, leaving traces: sticky spoons and fingerprints on the table, a smear on the refrigerator, the pot sitting on the stove. At least they'd remembered to turn the burner off under it, but it was coated with marshmallow. Charlotte scraped at it experimentally with her finger, but it had hardened past licking. She put the pot in the sink and ran hot water into it with a squirt of soap.

Chapter Twelve

SHE COULD HEAR ANDY BEFORE SHE COULD SEE HIM. SHE FOL-
lowed the dull, rhythmic sound of maul-head hitting iron
wedge: *Thunk. Thunk. Thunk.* There was an ear-shattering
ring when the log split through, a pause, then *thunk. Thunk.
Thunk.* Again. Andy was across the road beside the old barn.
In spite of the frost in the morning he was in shirt sleeves.
Next to him was a great heap of freshly split wood, and
against the barn a formidable pile of logs waiting. He swung
the maul easily, letting the weight of it do the work on the
way down.

Charlotte stood watching him in silence, unnoticed. He had
grown in the last year, not so much bigger—it was more as if
all the parts of him were catching up to each other, instead
of shooting off at different rates. He was broad-shouldered
and solid, used to hard physical work, like his father, who
wanted him to be anything but a farmer.

But it was all Andy wanted to do: cultivate his family's
land and grow things. Bit by bit he was wrestling back the
overgrown fields around the farmhouse. Three summers ago
he had cleaned out the little frame farm stand under the horse
chestnut tree opposite the barn and opened it for business
again. That was their first summer together: Kath and Andy,
Oliver and Charlotte. They had all worked at the farm.

It had been a fairly rocky few months, that vacation, and
by no means certain that they would become real friends:
each was difficult in his or her own way and each had a dif-

ferent reason for being there. Charlotte's and Oliver's motives were most similar: they sprang, not from a love for the land, but out of self-defense. It was Charlotte's first summer without Eliot and her parents had decided that she must *do* something with her vacation, not hang around limp and moping. Oliver's mother told him that if he couldn't find a good excuse for staying in Concord during the summer, he'd be packed off to camp or to Washington. They both realized, independently, that if they didn't take action themselves, their lives would be arranged for them by well-meaning adults—they would lose control.

Andy was only too happy to accept their offers of help; he needed everyone he could get, even the totally inexperienced. He alone knew the magnitude of what they were attempting, and it wasn't just a summer he was thinking about, it was his future. At thirteen, his father didn't think he was old enough to be serious. He thought three months of hard, unrewarding labor would convince Andy that farming wasn't worth it. The real arguments between them hadn't started. Andy had been then, and still was, dead serious about the farm. Charlotte had learned that for a fact long before Andy's father appeared to.

Kath at that time was still passionately, single-mindedly involved with horses, specifically the ones at Alan Watts's riding stables, not far from the farm. But whatever spare hours she had when she wasn't shoveling muck or cleaning tack or picking burrs out of horse tails, she devoted to her brother's project. When she made up her mind to do something she did it hard and determinedly. She and Andy had an unshakable loyalty to one another, a special relationship that Charlotte couldn't help envying. It had to do with being twins.

Looking back at herself and the others, Charlotte could see there were bound to have been problems. She, for one, had no idea what she was undertaking when she so blithely volunteered. She hadn't realized that farming meant long, hot, backbreaking hours every day, every week—that you couldn't stop and do something else, something frivolous, for a day or two when you felt like it. The only time she could remember Andy being genuinely angry with her was when she'd taken the Fourth of July weekend off without really saying. "You can't *run* a farm this way—it can't be just when you feel like it!" he'd exclaimed, angry and desperate. "You shouldn't have started if you didn't mean to keep coming. You shouldn't have let me count on you!" She couldn't defend herself against him, because she was beginning to see what it meant to him. It had been very sobering to come face to face with responsibility for the first time and to realize that accepting it meant loss of freedom. She had fought against that. She was still fighting it, each summer, when she gave up her vacation for Andy.

Between Oliver and Kath that first year there was almost constant friction. They had one spectacular fight about who was going to pick beans when they ran out at the stand one very hot afternoon. Neither would take orders from the other, and that continued. But once everyone recognized that fact, they found ways around it.

Oliver proved himself very clever at handling the business side of the operation: advertising and cash-flow and sales. He'd managed to get them featured, with photographs, in the *Concord Journal*, summer before last, and that had done wonders for their trade. Last year he had negotiated a deal with a natural foods restaurant in Lexington. Deb had put him onto the two women who ran the place. It was pretty nearly more success than they could handle. If the restaurant had been any bigger they wouldn't have been able to keep up with its demands. But Andy was determined to meet the challenge, and somehow they did.

Each year he expanded his fields and increased his crops. He always did half again as much work as anyone else. Even when last summer he felt financially secure enough to hire four extra workers—including his younger brother Dan, who, hard-nosed as he was, maintained you didn't value what you didn't pay for—that didn't mean there was less work to do; what it meant to Andy was that they could accomplish more.

Charlotte felt guilty for wishing they had more time for other things: picnics, hot sandy days at the beach, canoeing, bicycling out to Bates' Farm for ice cream cones, just *playing*.

She knew Andy was counting on her—on all of them—he made no secret of how much he needed them, and she hated the thought of letting him down. But she had trouble subduing a sense that she was missing out on things and regret for her lost irresponsibility. Still, she did it.

But what about next summer, she wondered, as she watched Andy hefting the maul. The pattern would be broken: Oliver would be missing. It would be like last Sunday afternoon, when he'd decided to leave, but it would go much deeper; it would force them all to change. Past Andy's shoulders, Charlotte looked across the snowy sloping fields, to the little pond and the dark line of trees beyond. The ice had not been cleared after last night's snowfall, but there was a clearly trodden path leading down from the road, and squinting against the glare, she could pick out two figures moving through the whiteness, one quite small and wearing a red jacket and hat. They were moving away, along the edge of the trees, scattering cracked corn, she guessed, for the squirrels and pheasants and anything else that would eat it. They'd be coming back soon and she wanted to talk to Andy first.

"Andy?" She went closer.

He missed his aim and knocked the wedge askew.

"Sorry."

"So'm I," he said without turning and without putting the maul down. She didn't think they meant the same thing. She went around the pile of split wood to where she could see his face. His rusty hair was damp on his forehead, his cheeks flushed with exertion and the cold, his breath smoked. She thrust her hands deep in her pockets, not sure what to say, remembering Pat's warning.

"Do you mind if I don't stop? It gets cold when I do," he said.

She nodded.

With the maul he straightened the wedge, then drove it through. The log split clean; he picked up the two halves. "Oak. Can you smell it?"

"It's sour," said Charlotte. The wood was pink inside, with a white edge under the bark.

"It's good," said Andy. He selected another log and set the

wedge carefully on the grain. "How's Oliver?"

"He seems all right. It's hard to tell," she answered carefully.

"I know." *Thunk. Thunk. Thunk.*

"It wasn't bad, you know. I mean for Commodore Shattuck. The doctor told my father he just went to sleep. He was even in bed." She watched him; he'd caught his lower lip between his teeth. "He wasn't sick, or in pain, Andy. He probably didn't even know when it happened." That was what everyone seemed to think was important. She offered it to him as comfort.

"Did you see him?" There was a spot of blood where he'd bitten too hard.

"No. But Oliver did. He was there with him when it—when he died. It was very sudden. Last Sunday, after we left here, I stopped on the way home and Commodore Shattuck was fine. Really he was."

Andy dropped the maul and rubbed his hands across his face, raking his fingers through his wiry hair. To her dismay, Charlotte saw tears in his eyes. "I can't believe it though," he said in a rough voice. "I just can't. I don't want it to be true, Charlie. I want him to be there now, like always. Why couldn't we have gone tobogganing today the way we planned, the way we did before, instead of this?"

"I don't know." She wished she knew what to say to him; she almost wished she hadn't come, but that was only because she didn't know the right thing to do. All she could think of to say was, "You better put your jacket on."

But he didn't seem to hear her; he turned his head away, but not before she saw he was actually crying. For a moment she froze, helpless. "Andy?" He stuck his hands in the rear pockets of his jeans and shook his head back fiercely. She forgot her awkwardness in an uprush of sympathy for him. She picked his jacket off the woodpile and put it over his shoulders.

"I—I'm sorry. I can't help it," he said, bleak and embarrassed. "Kath didn't cry."

"Neither did Oliver."

"He wouldn't let you see him do it," said Andy, making a face.

"It doesn't matter," said Charlotte. "I don't mind." They were standing very close. Andy took her hand in his cold, calloused one and gripped it hard. She thought, this is what should have happened with Oliver, only Oliver wouldn't let anyone near him. He lived beneath the surface, Andy lived on top. She and Andy could share, could comfort one another. "It's so strange," she said hesitantly, "to think of someone being alive one minute, and—and not the next. But that's all it is, just a minute's difference."

"What do you think has happened to him?" said Andy, sounding a little unsteady. "Where do you think he is?"

She hadn't thought about that. "I don't know. Somewhere better, I guess," she hazarded. "At least, that's what we're supposed to believe, isn't it? That when you die, if you've lived a good life, it's your reward."

"You think he's gone to heaven then?" said Andy quite seriously.

Charlotte hedged. "I don't know about heaven exactly. That sounds like angels and pink clouds. I don't think I believe in that, do you?"

Troubled, he shook his head. "No."

"Well," said Charlotte, "it seems to me that if you aren't here anymore, and you don't go somewhere else, you must just stop being altogether. You just live, and then you stop living. And then is there nothing? Can there be nothing?" The thought spread before her, a great black void.

Andy looked away, over the shining fields, his fingers tight around hers. "The trouble is," he said slowly, feeling his way, "that I don't understand how there can be somewhere better, Charlie. I mean better than here. This is what I want—right here. Commodore Shattuck loved it as much as I do, I'm sure he did. But he's been taken away from it. You said he didn't even know. I think that makes it worse. He wasn't like my grandfather, hurting all the time and not able to get out of bed. Or like his friend Ophelia Wardlaw who's forgotten where she is and what year she's in and who the people around her are. That's different. If you're suffering it's different. But he wasn't. How can that be a reward? To have to leave?"

"Andy, the world isn't perfect," objected Charlotte. "You can't say it is. It could be better in lots of ways."

But he shook his head. "It's *us* that could be better. The world's fine. Look at it, the way the parts fit together, Charlie, how it all works." He was full of his idea, intense with the effort of trying to express it to her. "Right now the ground's frozen solid and covered with snow. It looks as if nothing's alive, right? In another month though there'll be a thaw—there always is. The sap starts to run. Then you'll see green in the bushes and the maples showing red, and the new grass will start coming through the dead brown stuff. The birds will come and start singing. Our woodcocks will be down in the field again, like last year, showing off. You come and see. Then it'll be time to plant seeds. We don't make any of it happen. It happens because it does, not because of us. It's wonderful, you know that? But Commodore Shattuck won't be here for any of it this time. Not the geese flying in, or the ice breaking up and the willows turning yellow. He'll miss all those things, and he loved them."

"You don't know that," said Charlotte, uncertain. "Maybe wherever he is, he can still see all of it." She meant them to be comforting, but the words sounded tentative, unconvincing. What did happen? How could you ever know?

Andy stood looking at her, his eyes doubtful, but before he could say anything, Alice came floundering around the barn, followed by Kath and Paddy. Andy didn't think to unlock Charlotte's hand; she saw Kath register the fact that he was holding it, then look quickly away.

"Hey, Charlie!" cried Paddy. "I can make snow angels. Want to see?" Without waiting for a response, she flung herself on her back in a path of unmarked snow and waved her arms and legs up and down violently, showering Alice with white clots. Alice barked crossly and backed out of range. Paddy struggled up again, leaving great holes in the shape she'd made. "See? It's an angel. There's its wings, and there's its dress."

"Yes," said Charlotte, "I can see." She avoided looking at Kath, aware of a discordance among the three of them, as if someone had just played a wrong note. Gently, she disengaged her hand.

"I'll teach you. You want me to teach you? It's easy."

"You're getting snow all over the woodpile," said Andy abruptly, "and I bet your boots are full. Ma will throw a fit if you catch cold again. Come on, it must be about lunchtime." He took Paddy by one of her blue mittens. "What did you see down the hill? Pheasants?"

"No, but Alice chased a rabbit. I'm not going to let her come next time. I'm going to take carrots and lettuce. Maybe the rabbit will come to me, do you think it will, Andy? Come right up to me? If I sit very still?"

"It might." They started toward the house, leaving Kath and Charlotte to follow.

"Oliver didn't come," said Kath flatly, after a minute.

Charlotte shook her head, feeling ill at ease, and wondering what Kath made of finding her holding hands with Andy. But Kath was preoccupied with other things.

"He's not mad, is he?"

"Mad? Oliver? Why would he be?" She glanced at Kath with surprise.

Kath scowled fiercely. "At me. For yesterday when I came to your house. He didn't like it, I could tell. It's just—I *had* to know."

"Of course he's not mad at you." Charlotte thought it likely that Oliver had forgotten the episode almost as soon as it was over, but she didn't say so.

"You sure? I mean, I could apologize if it would make any difference."

"There's nothing to apologize *for*," said Charlotte impatiently. "All you did was come to see what was the matter. You're a friend of his, for pete's sake. Why should you apologize for that?" She couldn't understand what Kath was getting at. If anything, it seemed to her that Kath had a right to be annoyed with Oliver for the way he'd behaved, but she wouldn't say that to Kath.

"Do you know what's going to happen?"

"To Oliver? He'll go live with his mother in Washington. That's what Mom says."

"But he hates her!"

"He doesn't hate her, they just don't get along very well."

"What's the difference?" said Kath passionately. "It isn't fair. He shouldn't have to go if he doesn't want to."

Charlotte found she didn't want to discuss this right now; she didn't want to think about it. And she was unprepared for the strength of Kath's feelings on the subject. Crossly, she said, "Well he can't live by himself. And even if he could, the house doesn't belong to him—it was the Commodore's. Mom says it'll be sold. Where would he stay?"

"With you," said Kath unexpectedly. In a desperate rush she went on, "You've got lots of room in your house. More than we have. You don't use it all, you know you don't. Ma might even let him come here, at least until the end of school, we could manage. He shouldn't leave in the middle of the year."

"But—" said Charlotte. It was obvious that Kath had been thinking hard about all this.

"Do you want him to go?" she demanded.

"Of course not, but I don't see—"

Kath stopped in the middle of the snowy road and swung to face her. "He'd stay with you—he would. And I bet his mother would agree—she knows your family. I can ask Ma, I could get her to say yes—I'm pretty sure I could, but he wouldn't come here, not really. It isn't what he's used to. There're too many of us and not enough space. He doesn't like being crowded, I know that. But at least I'd *try*. He'll be miserable in Washington. It'll be awful."

Charlotte regarded her with a troubled frown. "Washington isn't that far away, Kath. It really isn't. Think how much worse it would be if Oliver had to go live with his father in California. We'll see him again."

"*You* will," said Kath bitterly. "I bet I—we won't. It's not going to be the same at all anymore. Anyhow, forget it. Forget the whole thing, will you? Forget I said anything." She gave Charlotte an anguished look, then turned and practically ran toward the house, as if appalled by what she'd said.

Charlotte stood staring after her, making no move to follow. Even with other people around, she did not want to be in Kath's company just then, and she suspected that Kath wouldn't want her there. She had exposed herself too thoroughly, laid her feelings bare. And Charlotte was swept with a tide of desolation. Kath was right: it wasn't going to be the same anymore.

Without consciously deciding to, she began to walk back along Sandy Pond Road, past the farmhouse, heading for home. Kath, of all people. Kath who was blunt and unsophisticated, scornful of the social graces, who reserved her attention for horses and showed not the slightest interest in boys as boys. Or at least she hadn't before this. Except the dance. And Charlotte saw her in a white ruffled blouse, her cheeks pink with effort, tentative, smiling, red hair glowing around her face. She wondered if Oliver had any idea. She didn't think so, she didn't think he could. Poor Kath. But even as Charlotte sympathized, she knew she wouldn't be the one to tell him.

"Hey!" called Andy, leaning out of the window of his mother's enormous old car, startling Charlotte out of her skin. "What happened? Why'd you leave like that? I thought you'd come in and have lunch with us, didn't you want to? You didn't even say goodbye." He sounded hurt.

"You almost gave me a heart attack, Andy Schuyler," she said crossly. "I didn't hear you, I was thinking about something. I—I have to get home."

"That's what you said last Sunday. But at least you told me you were going then. Why do you have to get home, Charlie? I thought maybe we could—you know—take a walk somewhere at least. In the Town Forest, or at Mount Misery, or Walden."

"I can't." Her heart had almost slowed to normal and she was sorry she'd snapped at him. It would have been a good afternoon to walk, brittle and clear, with the sun tracing blue shadows on the snow, and Andy for company. "It's the interment," she explained, the word feeling strange in her

III

mouth. "It's this afternoon and I'm supposed to go."

"Oh." He couldn't argue. "Well, I can take you home, can't I?"

She smiled at him. "Thanks."

It was a silent drive. Several times she was afraid he was going to ask again why she had left so abruptly; he glanced over at her and she could see the question in his face, but she didn't acknowledge it. Let Kath explain. But when they got to the Paige house, Andy pulled up at the curb in front.

"I won't come in," he said, "to see Oliver. Unless you think I should? I'm not good at this kind of thing," he added unhappily. "I only make it worse. You know."

"It's all right," she told him. "I don't even know that Oliver's home." Or what sort of mood he's in, she added to herself. She didn't want to go through a repetition of the day before, not with Andy.

"Tell him—tell him I'm sorry, will you?" Andy gripped the steering wheel.

"Yes." She opened the door and got out.

"Charlie, you won't—will you tell him—about what I said to you? I mean, I haven't worked it out very well. It must have sounded pretty—"

"No," she said, "I won't."

He nodded, relieved. "Will you be at school Monday?"

"I don't know. Oliver's mother is coming Monday and Tuesday's the memorial service. There's a lot to do. Thanks for bringing me home, Andy. I'm sorry about today. I'll see you." She waved until he was out of sight.

Chapter Thirteen

FORTIFIED WITH A HEARTY MIDDAY DINNER, SUNDAY AFTER-noon Charlotte, Oliver, Mrs. Paige, and Jean drove to the Commodore's house to see what needed to be done to clean out the kitchen and collect Oliver's belongings. They left Max and Mr. Paige nominally in charge of two-year-old Hilary. Actually Max was stretched out on the couch, while Hilary's grandfather played peek-a-boo with her.

"Don't you dare go to sleep and leave your father alone in her clutches, Max," warned Jean severely.

"Nonsense. What do we need him for?" said Mr. Paige, on his hands and knees. "Don't you worry about us." Hilary's head popped around the big green chair; she let out a de-lighted shriek as Mr. Paige growled and waggled his eye-brows at her. Max groaned and opened one eye. "All right, all right, don't glare at me like that. How can I sleep with this going on anyway?"

"I honestly don't know," replied Jean, "but you've done it before, my love."

"And don't you get her too excited, Gordon, or she'll never calm down again," said Mrs. Paige.

"Oh, just go away and leave us alone, will you? Bunch of spoil sports!"

Hilary had silky red-gold hair, round, round cheeks, and a wicked grin. She was curious about everything within her ever-increasing grasp and objected strenuously to having her self-education curtailed, as it often was, abruptly and for very good reasons. For so small a person, she could produce what Charlotte considered a mind-blowing volume of sound. When she came to visit in Concord, the cats melted silently into the background, leaving not so much as a grin. Poor old Camomile had been jolted out of a placid middle-age when Hilary began to crawl, and now spent her days in Max and Jean's Cambridge apartment living on the tops of bureaus, bookcases, and windowsills, when she wasn't upstairs seeking refuge with the two graduate student tenants. Hilary made life lively.

As they pulled out of the driveway, Jean sank back in her seat with a sigh of relief. "I feel guilty about foisting her off on Gordon that way," she admitted. "Max isn't going to be any help, I'm afraid. He's been working fearful hours on this hospital proposal. I hardly ever see him these days, and when I do, his eyes are invariably closed. He can sleep through practically anything."

"He always could," said Charlotte. "He always used to sleep through his station on the train from Cambridge and wake up at the end of the line in Acton and have to come back again. He used to fight with them because they charged him extra. He said if they wanted him to get off, they could wake him up, but they never did."

"He never told me that," said Jean with a chuckle. "I just hope Hilary doesn't wear her granddad to a frazzle."

"That's what granddads are for," said Mrs. Paige. "In case you hadn't noticed, he's absolutely besotted with her, anyway."

"He really is, isn't he? She's got him in the palm of her sticky little hand."

"Speaking of which, I was surprised she didn't lose one when she put her fingers in Amos's mouth." Mrs. Paige glanced in the rearview mirror. "I confess I stopped breathing. He was the model of restraint, Oliver."

"He's a good dog," said Oliver. "He's got a better temper than I have." He rubbed Amos between the ears and Amos slapped a moist kiss on his forehead. He was wedged between Charlotte and Oliver on the back seat, sitting up straight and alert. He loved riding in cars.

Oliver had refused to leave him behind, and Charlotte, fond as she was of her niece, agreed with him. For once her sympathies were with Amos. Far from being intimidated by such a large, miscellaneous dog, Hilary had been enchanted by him. She had thrown herself on him with cries of joy before anyone could move fast enough to catch her, and Amos, with a martyred expression on his homely gray face, had borne her very physical attentions like a lamb in wolf's clothing. Oliver came to his rescue before things went too far. Hilary was indignant, Amos abjectly grateful. "You ought to teach her not to do that. Dogs aren't toys," he'd said. And Jean agreed, taking no offense, though privately Charlotte suspected they didn't have the same reason in mind.

Even though the Commodore's house had only been empty since Thursday, it felt unlived-in to Charlotte. Like a clock that had run down and been forgotten, its hands set at a time that had gone past.

"Goodness, it's very tidy," said Mrs. Paige, looking around the kitchen.

"Of course it is," said Oliver. "Why wouldn't it be?"

"No reason, Oliver," she said quickly, "it's just that—"

"You expect things to be different," said Charlotte, coming to her mother's rescue.

"They are. But we always kept the house neat. I think, if you don't mind, I'll go and pack my clothes. Come on, Amos."

"Put my foot in it," said Mrs. Paige wryly when they'd gone. "I'm sorry."

"Where should we begin?" asked Jean. "The refrigerator, I suppose. And we'll have to check the cupboards for perishables."

"Perishables?" echoed Charlotte, struck by the word.

"Anything that would attract mice, for a start—cereal, crackers, flour, sugar," said her mother, taking off her coat and beginning to open doors. "They're very well stocked." The shelves were lined with canned goods arranged in categories: fruit, vegetables, soup, tuna fish, baked beans, stew. "You can stack these in one of the cartons, Charlotte."

"But they won't spoil," she objected.

"There's no point in leaving them here, darling. No one

will be living in the house for a long time. The rector at Trinity suggested we could give things like canned goods to the church to be distributed to people who need them. Sam would have been glad to have us do that, don't you think?"

Helplessly, Charlotte nodded. She hadn't realized how very much she would dislike this. It felt like prying, in spite of knowing that he was dead and none of it would bother him. Jean, hunting for plastic bags in the drawers, discovered a nearly-full bag of Tootsie Rolls, tucked under a pile of clean dish towels: a cache. Charlotte knew she and the Commodore shared a weakness for sweets, and Oliver was as hard on his great-uncle as Deb was on Charlotte. "Because," he explained with exaggerated patience when Charlotte accused him of being mean, "his doctor said sugar isn't good for him. I wouldn't care otherwise." She pictured Commodore Shattuck hiding the Tootsie Rolls from his great-nephew, sneaking a couple now and then, probably enjoying them twice as much as if he'd been able to eat them openly. She wondered who had bought them for him and smuggled them in so Oliver wouldn't know.

"Isn't there something else I can do?" she asked desperately.

"What?"

"How about wastebaskets," suggested Jean. "They need to be emptied. Charlie, do you know where the trash barrel is?"

Gratefully, she escaped. Emptying trash was a normal sort of chore; she did it at home every week. But as she worked her way through the downstairs rooms, she understood more and more clearly that nothing in this house was normal any more.

The Commodore had filled it with himself, furnished it with his possessions: things he had gathered around him during a lifetime that carried messages and associations only he could decipher. Without him, they lost their meaning and became simply objects. For the first time she noticed how shabby much of the furniture looked. In the dining room one of the glass panes in the china cupboard was cracked, and the knobs were darkened with years of handling. There was a pale, threadbare depression in the carpet under the table where the Commodore's feet had always rested; the plank-bottomed chairs didn't match, and the painted ones were chipped and scraped and showed different colors underneath the top layer of finish.

It was the same in the living room: a stain on the rug just inside the door where Amos had made an early mistake. The bright embroidered cushions didn't hide the fact that the old brown sofa was fraying around the edges and the piping had come loose on one arm. There were scratches on the coffee table, of different shades and ages, and a large blanched ring where something wet had stood. It had always tilted to the left, that table; there were several matchbook covers under one of its legs to balance it. These had all been such small, unimportant things, as long as the Commodore was there.

As she crossed to the wastebasket by the fireplace, she noticed a scatter of dark burn marks on the hearth rug, some of them quite big. They obviously predated the electric heater that stood in the opening. She knew the heater was little more than a year old—it had been Oliver's present to his great-uncle two Christmases ago. To save lugging firewood and cleaning up after it, he said. The Commodore had always loved a good cheerful fire, but he had been surprisingly acquiescent about the heater. At the time she thought it was because Oliver had given it to him, but now she looked at the charred spots and wondered. The electric heater didn't spit sparks into the room. You could go to sleep in front of it without fear of setting the house ablaze. Or you could let your great-uncle go to sleep in front of it without worrying that the house might burn down in your absence.

She stared at the hearth rug, troubled, no longer seeing it. He had aged in the three years she'd known him. She'd noticed it the last time they'd been in this room together—barely a week ago. The Commodore had looked tired and old in a way she hadn't been conscious of before. Or had she seen it and ignored it? When you looked at people who were familiar to you, did you see them as they were, or as you expected to see them? Like Kath, who had surprised her so much the day before. She'd gotten used to seeing her in a certain way, but she'd changed. And Commodore Shattuck—ought she to have been alert to what was happening to him sooner? But what had happened, actually? He wasn't sick, she was sure of that. Oliver badgered his great-uncle about 'flu shots and physical checkups, not going out in bad weather, taking his medication. The Commodore grumbled and complained, but Oliver persisted.

No. Commodore Shattuck had simply gotten old, gotten slower, sometimes forgetful, less energetic. No one could do anything about that, not Oliver, not Charlotte, not her parents, not the doctor, not even the Commodore himself. It happened to everyone.

Standing there, clutching the wastebasket, she wondered what he had noticed himself. Had he thought about being old, about dying? Did you, when you got to be his age, or did you try not to? What had he believed about death? Had he felt, as Andy did, that the world was too good to leave? Did he believe in something, or in nothing? Could she possibly have been right—was he aware right now that she was standing there in his living room, wondering?

"Charlotte?" Her mother's voice shook her out of her immobilizing thoughts. "Haven't you finished?" Mrs. Paige asked. "What have you been doing, darling? Jean and I are almost done in here." They had filled five cartons, two canvas bags, and a large plastic trash bag. Jean was sponging out the empty refrigerator.

"Sorry. I haven't been upstairs yet. I was—thinking."

"Well, you can go see how Oliver's getting along and hurry him a little, while we start carrying these to the car," said her mother briskly.

As the kitchen door swung behind her, Charlotte heard her say, "I had no idea I'd find this so depressing, Jean. I'll be glad to be done."

Jean's answer was inaudible, then Mrs. Paige's reply: "I don't know. I hope not, but perhaps I shouldn't have sent her up alone. He is so unemotional, Jean, I don't know what to think. He must be feeling *some*thing. I'm sure he and Sam were fond of each other—after all, Sam gave him a home. But he just doesn't crack, that boy—not even yesterday, at the grave. He stood there without showing anything. I hope Paula knows what to do—he concerns me. Poor Charlotte, she isn't—"

Whatever her mother thought she wasn't, Charlotte didn't wait to hear. True, she had wept a little at the burial, but the tears weren't grief so much as weariness and strain, reaction to life rather than death, not that she had tried to explain. The interment itself had been unemotional and brief: a few words said by Reverend Francks by the side of a neat rectangular hole—Charlotte kept wondering how they had cut it out of the frozen cemetery—the plain oblong coffin lowered in, then covered over with earth; flowers looking garish and out of place in the austere, wintry landscape. There were only the handful of them: the Paiges and Charlotte, Oliver, Reverend Francks and three men to do the actual work. There was no sign of the Commodore, just the box. Then it was over and she was relieved; she did not want to dwell on it.

Oliver's door stood partly open: she glimpsed neat piles of folded clothing on his bed and a suitcase open on the floor, but she couldn't detect any movement. Hesitantly, she put her head into the room. Oliver was sitting on one of his window seats, his forehead against the glass, looking out at the street. Amos's gray head rested on his knee. Charlotte withdrew and knocked to announce herself.

There was a pause, then he said, "What?"

"It's me. Mom and Jean have finished in the kitchen. They sent me to see how you're doing."

"Not very well." He sighed. "I got sidetracked."

"So did I," she admitted, but he didn't seem to hear her. Gently he removed Amos's head from his leg and stood up. There was a damp mark on his trousers. "It won't take me much longer, just putting the rest in suitcases."

"You don't have to take everything with you now, you know. You can always come back again."

Oliver looked around the room. "I don't think I want to. Not for a while anyway. I was reminding myself of the view," he said unemotionally. "I'll miss it—the river and the Buttrick house up on the hill."

Charlotte swallowed hard; she felt like crying again.

"What will happen to all his things, Oliver? I mean the special ones—the paintings and books, and the—all that up in the attic?" She couldn't help thinking of the yard sale they had helped to organize for the Commodore's elderly friends, the Wardlaw sisters. That had been over a year ago, in the fall, after Ophelia had broken her hip. Viola had decided they would have to sell their house, the home they had shared for more than fifty years. Their doctor said Ophelia would never be well enough again to leave the nursing home, and Viola couldn't stay on alone. She had moved into one of the tiny apartments attached to the home, cramming it with those possessions she couldn't bear to part with. Everything else had been sold or given to Goodwill. Charlotte, Oliver, Andy, and Kath had run the sale. Viola didn't want to watch strangers picking over their belongings, so the Commodore had taken her out for lunch, to the Wayside Inn.

"It depends on Uncle Sam's will," said Oliver matter-of-factly. "I was thinking about the paintings—I know they aren't masterpieces, but they aren't bad, either. And so many of them are of places in Concord. Would your father take them for the museum, do you suppose? They ought to be kept together."

"Oh, yes," said Charlotte. "I'm sure he would. That's a *good* idea."

Oliver went on deliberately piling his clothes in a suitcase, fitting them carefully. "I don't know what anyone will do about the attic," he said after a few minutes. "Even if you wanted to move it, how could you?"

"You could pack up all the little pieces," said Charlotte, "all the buildings and the ship models, anyway. They put so much love and work into it."

He shrugged. "They don't care anymore, and it would never mean the same to anyone else. Ophelia probably doesn't remember it, and Viola has no room in her apartment. Besides, as you said the first time Uncle Sam took you up to see it, the pleasure was in making it, not having it."

"Did I?" She was surprised.

Oliver nodded. "Uncle Sam agreed with you—I was quite jealous."

"Charlotte? Charlotte!" Mrs. Paige called up the stairs.

"I'm almost finished," said Oliver, hooking the straps over his shirts.

"Wait a minute." Charlotte darted out and halfway down the stairs to meet her mother.

"What's taking so long?" asked Mrs. Paige. "Is everything all right?" She sounded slightly anxious. "Do you need help, darling?"

"No, we're fine. It's just that Oliver doesn't want to come back again, so he's packing everything he wants to take."

"The car's pretty full now—is there a lot?"

"You could take the cartons to the church and come back for us," suggested Charlotte. "Or Max could."

Mrs. Paige looked at her hard. "I suppose that's possible—if you're sure that you're both all right. I don't like leaving you alone—"

"Really, it's fine," Charlotte assured her impatiently. "We'll be ready when you come back."

A few minutes later she and Oliver watched the Volvo back out of the driveway below. "I don't see why we need to stay," said Oliver, as he snapped shut the second suitcase. "I'm finished."

"It would have been a tight fit with Amos, too. Anyway, I wondered if—" She hesitated awkwardly. "—Well, if you'd mind if we went up to the attic. We haven't been up in ages, and I'd like to see it again."

"No one's been up for a long time. It's not heated, and the stairs are dangerous. All right. Amos, you'll have to stay, I don't want you squashing anything."

They left him sitting dejectedly at the bottom of the narrow little staircase. "I thought he did his painting up here, too," said Charlotte.

"He hadn't done any painting for more than a year. His hands weren't steady enough—he said it just frustrated him not to be able to make pictures come the way he planned them in his head. And nothing's been added to the model since before the Wardlaws moved. Uncle Sam said Viola hadn't the heart to think about it without Ophelia."

Oliver opened the trapdoor and a waterfall of frigid air

sluiced down on them, taking Charlotte's breath away. She pushed up through it as if she were swimming. The attic above was full of hard, cold winter sunshine. It came through the dormers in the roof; the glass in them looked as if it had been painted bright blue. The Commodore's attic was not used for storage space, it was the cellar that was piled with dusty miscellaneous clutter. Instead, spread out across the attic floor lay a miniature landscape, minutely detailed: papier-mâché hills, plowed fields made of corrugated cardboard, painted rivers and ponds, rutted sandy roads, stone walls built of pebbles, tiny animals, people, wagons and coaches, and scattered through this Lilliputian countryside, the farms and villages of colonial Massachusetts. It was a masterpiece of planning and execution. Charlotte felt the same wonder at the sight of it now that she had the first time she'd set eyes on it.

The Wardlaw sisters had begun the whole thing years and years ago with a model of the Old North Bridge, complete with tiny soldiers and Minutemen, for the three hundred and twenty-fifth anniversary of the founding of the town. It had been displayed on a large table in the library foyer, marveled at and photographed, visited by school children, featured in the paper, until the library needed its space back and the Wardlaws had to find another home for it. Commodore Shattuck offered them space in his attic, where he had his studio, and once the Bridge was installed up there, surrounded by all that empty floor, the rest began to grow around it, little by little: first Concord town, then Lexington, Bedford, Lincoln, Carlisle, Walden Pond. It crept gradually eastward toward the sea, consuming the attic floor, all the way to Boston Harbor, painted deep blue-green with flecks of white. The Wardlaws' father, Jonathan, had been a builder of model ships in his time, and they contributed his miniature sailing ships, cutting the bottoms off with great care so they seemed to be floating.

Unfortunately there was no room to extend the arm of Cape Cod without building an addition to the house, but they spread south to Plymouth and north to the still-incomplete Salem. It had all been done for the fun of doing it—very few people even knew it existed. But Charlotte, gazing about, could not imagine taking it apart and turning the attic back into an ordinary attic. "What'll you do?" she asked Oliver at last.

"I don't know." His voice was angry. "It shouldn't be my responsibility. I shouldn't have to do anything with it."

"But you can't just leave it. You don't know who will live here next."

"So? Let them worry about it. Their kids can play with it."

"It's not a toy," said Charlotte, shocked.

"What is it then? Why shouldn't someone get some fun out of it? Have you got a better idea?"

"But—"

"What do you think people are going to say when they find out about it? What would my mother think?" He gave a humorless little laugh. "She'd think that Uncle Sam was senile."

"Lots of people build models," protested Charlotte. "Nobody's ever called the Wardlaws senile and they've been doing it for years quite openly."

Oliver shivered. "It's cold up here. Let's go downstairs and wait. I don't want to think about it anymore."

"But someone's going to have to," said Charlotte.

"Not me. Not right now." He secured the trapdoor behind them. Amos bumped awkwardly against their knees, lashing his tail back and forth and wiggling his ears. They carried the suitcases to the front door and put on their jackets, gloves, and scarves in silence. Oliver took his outdoor clothes out of the hall closet and made a bundle of them. After about ten minutes Max and Jean's old station wagon pulled into the driveway and they went out to it. Charlotte remembered that she had never finished her job: the upstairs wastebaskets hadn't been emptied. She didn't mention it.

123

Chapter Fourteen

ON MONDAY IT WAS UNDERSTOOD THAT THEY WOULD GO BACK to school. There was no reason for them not to; there was nothing for them to do at home except wait for the next thing to happen. Charlotte both dreaded and looked forward to being back in class: she was behind with her work from the week before and she knew people were going to ask awkward questions, but school would at least fill the day. She did not want to sit around the house with Oliver, waiting for his mother and stepfather to arrive.

At breakfast, Oliver suggested that he drive the Commodore's car to school. Charlotte, watching her parents, saw them exchange dubious glances. "It's cold," said Oliver, "and the car ought to be used or it won't start. It's a bit temperamental."

"They won't let you park in the school lot, will they?" asked Mr. Paige.

"I have a parking sticker."

"Wel-l-l—" He sounded reluctant. "Kit? What do you think?"

"The roads are clear," said Mrs. Paige, obviously trying to make the best of it. "Just be careful, Oliver, it may be icy."

"Of course."

Charlotte was glad not to face the long, windy walk at either end of the day; the prospect of being driven appealed to her greatly. It also meant she could have a second cup of cocoa with tiny marshmallows without having to burn her tongue gulping it.

"Dress warmly," said Oliver as they went upstairs to collect their belongings.

"Why? We'll be in the car."

"Because it's cold, and it takes time for the heater to work. I'll go and start the engine. Meet you there."

Charlotte frowned thoughtfully after him, but bundled herself into the usual layers she wore for walking to school. He had taken the car out of the driveway and was waiting for her in front of the house, a plume of exhaust flickering from the tailpipe. He was impatient to be off and hardly gave her time to get her door closed before shifting into gear. His face, however, betrayed even less than usual, and his eyes were fixed on the road.

There was a red light at Sudbury Road; Oliver slowed and stopped for it. As he did so, like a jack-in-the-box, a large furry gray head thrust itself up between the two front seats. Charlotte gave a muffled cry of surprise. It was Amos, of course, but so unexpected that she couldn't help herself.

"Oliver! Why in the *world*—"

The light changed and the traffic moved forward. "I told you to stay *down*," said Oliver severely. "Get back and sit, Amos. *Sit*." Amos flattened his ears and looked woefully at Oliver, who continued to stare straight ahead. "Go on!" The dog withdrew, scrabbled onto the back seat, and sat.

"But what are you going to do with him?" demanded Charlotte. "You can't leave him in the car all day, it's too cold. And you can't take him to classes with you. This is ridiculous. He was much better off at home."

"It's all right," said Oliver. "I know what I'm doing."

"I doubt it," Charlotte muttered. She wondered fleetingly if he had temporarily lost his head, if something had slipped, and gave a little shiver.

They drove past the first entry road to the high school, avoiding the tangle of buses and students by the front door; the second road led directly to the parking lot. But Oliver drove past that one, too. Charlotte watched it go, turning her head in disbelief. "Hey!" was all she could manage to exclaim. Oliver kept his foot on the gas and Charlotte craned backwards stupidly. They pulled up at the traffic light at Route 2.

"What—where are you going? It's not that early, you know. We'll miss the first bell."

"And the second," said Oliver calmly, "and the third. Unless you want to get out here and walk back. You can. I won't stop you. But I'm not going to school."

She stared at him, trying to gauge his state of mind. This was no spur-of-the-moment decision; he'd planned this in advance, that was obvious—from Amos's presence in the back seat and his instructions to her to wear warm clothing.

"If you aren't going to come with us, you'd better get out now, the light's changing and I'm in the middle lane. I can't hold everyone up."

She made no move to open the door, and a minute later they drove on. He signaled and turned east on Route 2. He knew exactly what he was doing, where they were going, she realized. Alarm fizzed through her. "Oliver, you're not—are you—are you running away?" she asked in an odd, breathless voice.

"Of course not. Don't be silly. You should put your seat belt on."

She forced herself to move, to stack her books on the floor under her feet, and fastened the belt across her chest. Her brain wasn't processing any of this very well. Outside the car, the roadsides slid away; they left Concord behind. Oliver concentrated on the traffic, which was thick with commuters heading to work in Cambridge and Boston and the sprawling plants along Route 128. Amos sat upright in back, his nose pressed to the window, quivering and making excited little whurps through his closed jaws. Oliver had expended a lot of time and patience in getting him to stop leaping from side to side and barking at everything that moved. Occasionally still he forgot himself, and his deep bass voice was deafening in an enclosed space. But at the moment he was doing his best to behave.

At last Charlotte took a deep, nearly steady breath and

pulled herself together. "What happens when they miss us?"

"Nothing. They'll suppose we stayed home again, that's all. Your parents are both at work, and they'll assume we're at school."

"But if you aren't running away—why aren't we going to school? Why didn't you tell me before? Where are we going?"

He shook his head. "Too many questions. Just wait."

When they got to Route 128, he turned north. The traffic was just as heavy, but now laced with enormous container trucks whining along the highway at frightening speed. The Commodore's little car rocked every time one passed, slamming the displaced air into it. Charlotte hung onto the edge of her seat. Ordinarily she would not have been scared, but she was still grappling with the drastic, unexpected change in her plans for the day. She felt as if everything had suddenly plunged out of control. They couldn't have extricated themselves from the fury of cars and trucks hurtling them along if they had wanted; they were trapped. She was trapped.

Gradually her panic waned, and she relaxed a little—enough to notice that although Oliver's hands were steady on the wheel, he was gripping it hard enough to make his knuckles white. Paradoxically that made her relax still further. He wasn't as calm as he appeared; there were things working under that smooth exterior. It cost her a tremendous amount of willpower, but she kept still, not asking the questions that were exploding inside her head like fireworks.

Amos, however, couldn't hold himself in any longer and barked as a trailer of new cars snarled past, and Oliver jumped. Charlotte felt the car wiggle. She twisted around under her seat belt and concentrated on keeping the dog quiet. He covered her hands with wet kisses, his tail thumped the seat. She wondered where she would have a chance to wash off the dog spit.

Oliver took the exit for Maine and New Hampshire, and traffic thinned almost at once as they headed away from the cities. After a few miles Oliver's fingers loosened. "I've never driven at rush hour before," he admitted.

"Terrific," said Charlotte dryly.

"We're all right, aren't we?" he retorted.

"You kidnapped me."

"I did not. You could have gotten out and gone to school. I wouldn't have stopped you."

Something suddenly occurred to her. "Did you want me to? Would you rather I hadn't come with you?" He hadn't had much choice. It would have been really peculiar if he'd driven to school alone.

He gave a little shrug. "I don't mind."

His apparent indifference stung. "I can sit in the back seat and you can pretend I'm not here at all," she replied frostily. "If you'd told me before, I would have walked to school."

"Don't be a pain. If I'd wanted to get away alone I'd have figured out how to do it."

She knew he would have. "All right," she said grudgingly, "but why are we going? Is it just to avoid people? You know, sooner or later—"

"Come on, Charlotte, don't you give me that stuff!" He sounded angry. "No, that isn't the reason. And even if it was, I *won't* have to face them sooner or later, not those kids. This would have been my last day at school there—didn't you think of that? Tomorrow's the service, and Wednesday—Wednesday I'll be gone."

Cold, she looked out the window. Wednesday, the day after tomorrow. She hadn't allowed herself to think about it. She saw Kath, desperate, in the middle of the road, urging her to get her mother to let Oliver stay in Concord. *Kath* had thought about it. She felt hollow inside. Suppose Oliver had taken Kath with him today instead of her? Never mind the logistics, just suppose . . . She tore herself away from the thought. He hadn't. Never mind it, she didn't want to think about Kath.

Oliver followed the signs to Newburyport. It was an old seacoast town, prosperous in the days of sailing ships. Its wide main street was lined with enormous, square, imposing sea captains' houses, some of them grown shabby around the edges, each with a wooden widow's walk on top like a coronet, where the women had stood to watch for their husbands' ships. Charlotte had always fancied a widow's walk in much the same way that she coveted the window seats in Oliver's bedroom at the Commodore's house. They seemed terribly romantic to her.

On the east side of the town, between it and the Atlantic Ocean, lay a long, narrow sandy strip of land called Plum Island. It was a National Wildlife Refuge, all but the ends where there were clusters of summer cottages elbowing each other for a few square feet of the limited ground. The middle part of the island was empty: acres of beach plum, salt roses, and poison ivy, with pale, heaving dunes and a windy beach on one side, and marshy flats grown over with salt hay and cattails on the other.

In summer, Newburyport swarmed with tourists, vacationers, and beach people. Locked in winter, it was very different: austere and quiet, going about its real life. Oliver pulled up by the snowy common and reached for the map in the glove compartment.

"If you want to get to the beach," said Charlotte, "you go up to the traffic light and turn left, then right at the end of the street, past the airfield and across the bridge."

Oliver didn't like being told. He gave her a sharp look, but put the map away again. "How do you know it so well?"

"Eliot and I used to come up here a lot. It was one of our favorite places. If you go left here instead of right, you come to a terrific bakery," she added hopefully.

"It's only nine-thirty, you can't be hungry already."

"Quarter of ten. And if we're going to walk on the beach I will be hungry. It really is good."

"I suppose Eliot took you there."

She nodded. "What's wrong with that?"

"Nothing," he said moodily.

They bought four Danish pastries and six elephant ears from an unsmiling gray-haired man who eyed them suspiciously, doubtless wondering why they weren't in school. Oliver paid; he seemed to have an inexhaustible supply of money, still the Commodore's, Charlotte supposed, although she didn't want to ask. There really was no reason to feel odd about spending it—as Oliver had said earlier, the Commodore could have no use for it. She was glad to leave the shop in spite of its warm, sweet smell. "You have expensive tastes," said Oliver as they got back into the car.

"You didn't have to buy them," she snapped.

He said nothing. She began to wish she had gotten out of the car back in Concord when he'd given her the chance. If he was going to be like this all day, she didn't see why he had wanted company.

Things had been very different when they had come to Plum Island the last time, in August, early one hot Sunday morning. There had been six of them crammed into Pat Schuyler's station wagon, which Skip had borrowed for the expedition. He'd agreed to drive as long as Deb came too. It had been a mighty struggle to tear her away from the store and Andy from the farm, but in the end they had persevered.

That had been a lovely day, stolen from the routine of farm work, free and lazy. The sun blazed overhead making the sand shimmer with heat, and the dark blue sea crunched and mumbled the beach with deceptive benevolence—deceptive because even on the hottest days it was blood-curdlingly cold. If you waded in slowly you were likely to wade back out again before the waves rose above your knees. The best way was to race down the sand shouting and leap in all at once, without stopping to notice. It was like having someone punch you in the stomach.

They had a picnic and lay about on towels and beachcombed and buried Andy up to the neck in sand. On the way home, they wandered the back roads through Ipswich, Rowley, and Wenham, singing silly songs: "Ninety-Nine Bottles of Beer on the Wall," and "Found a Peanut," and "I Know an Old Lady Who Swallowed a Fly," and stopped twice for ice cream. Deb had made a token protest, but gave in because she said she didn't want to spoil their fun. Skip commended her for pretending to enjoy her fudge sundae so convincingly.

"What are you smiling at?" Oliver interrupted her thoughts.

"I was just remembering when we came up here last summer. Skip got so terribly sunburned, and I dropped the chicken in the sand and we had to wash it off in the sea, and Andy sang that awful song about ravioli, and—"

130

"Yes," Oliver cut her off. "I was there too. Let's not talk about it now."

"It's better than not talking about anything," she retorted. "What's the matter with you, anyway?"

"Nothing," he said coolly, "except that I wanted to get away for a while, and I didn't want to bring all those people along with us. I should have picked someplace you'd never been before. There isn't a whole lot of time left, Charlotte."

"You make it sound like the end of the world," she said.

"Nothing that spectacular or simple. That would take care of everybody's problems—even mine."

"Don't be silly." She hid her growing dismay with scorn.

"Look," said Oliver, "this isn't a picnic. I didn't bring you with me to have a good time. It isn't last summer anymore, everything's different now."

"You haven't yet told me why you did bring me. Maybe if you had I wouldn't have come."

His fingers were tight again on the steering wheel; he didn't look at her. "Maybe you wouldn't have. I thought you wanted to help. My mistake."

"Help *how?* You won't let me help. I don't know what you want!"

"If you'd just—just give me a chance," he said angrily. "You don't understand—"

Amos, distracted from the passing scene by what he detected in their voices, pushed his head between them, ears cocked anxiously, and gave a little whine.

"Amos, get *back!*" snapped Oliver. Amos hastily withdrew, looking abject.

"Don't yell at him, it isn't his fault," snapped Charlotte, defending Amos for the first time in their acquaintance. Oliver's eyes narrowed but he made no answer. Mutinously, she took the largest elephant ear out of the bakery bag and bit a chunk out of it.

In furious silence they drove out of town. The uneven row of summer houses at the rim of the harbor huddled derelict and cheerless under the hard sun, like flotsam thrown up by the sea. The airfield was deserted, shut for the season, but a wind sock on one of the rusty hangers stood out straight from its staff, indicating a brisk wind off the sea. Below the arched bridge the tidal river ran cold and black and the marsh was crusted with salt ice. There was no one in the warden's booth at the entrance to the refuge and only three cars parked in the main lot as they drove past. A little further along, Charlotte saw a knot of people gathered on the dike above the marsh, staring at something through telescopes and binoculars. Out of season, Eliot always said, it was a toss-up whether there were more birds or birdwatchers on Plum Island. Certainly no one else appeared to be around.

Oliver chose one of the small parking areas near the middle of the island and pulled in. Charlotte looked down at the crumbs in her lap and blamed him for the fact that she hadn't even tasted the pastry, much less enjoyed it. Ignoring her, he got out, opened the back door, and hooked Amos's leash. The dog bounded out joyfully, having forgotten the earlier unpleasantness, and tugged urgently to be away and exploring. All Oliver said to Charlotte was, "If you're coming, lock your door," before he set out on a path toward the beach. He didn't wait to see what she'd do, or look back before disappearing over the first dune. She stared after him and her eyes blurred with tears. Slowly she climbed out and followed, trying to blink them down, her feet clumsy in the sand.

It was all wrong with Oliver and she didn't understand why. Arguing was nothing new for them, they had argued with one another since the very beginning—the day they'd fallen in the duck pond together. All of them argued, even Andy once in a great while, although he hadn't the heart for it really. Then they made up again and went on from there. It was a measure of their friendship that there was room among them for disagreement without emnity. But this was different. She didn't see what she and Oliver were fighting about. What had happened should bring them closer, not push them apart. She ought to be comforting him and he should be allowing her to, not storming off alone, full of angry words. Why couldn't Oliver behave like Andy? But she knew the answer to that: because he wasn't Andy, he was another person altogether, and wishing wouldn't change him. She had come to realize that friendship was a matter of accepting the whole person, difficult as that might be, not picking out the bits you liked and discarding the rest. There were things about Andy that frustrated and annoyed her, too.

She heaved a great sigh. To her relief, the tears had drained back, leaving her unhappy but calm. She trudged through the sand valley between the dunes. There was no sign of either Oliver or Amos, and the sand was too soft to hold distinct prints. The scouring winds had blown away most of the snow close to the ocean; patches of it caught around bushes and in clumps of bleached grass and dents in the sand like a sprinkling of powdered sugar. Overhead the sky was pale frost-blue; gulls hung in the wind, sharp-eyed, moving only their heads. They were the only living things visible in the bleak landscape, though the sand was scattered with rabbit pellets.

At the top of the last dune the wind pounced on her, racing straight in over the tumbled sea, coarse as sandpaper. She gasped, then took a great aching lungful of it. There were a few dark, bundled figures walking above the wave line, quite far in the distance, and she picked out Amos, tearing in zigzags over the beach; she could feel his muscles stretching. But Oliver—she looked and didn't see him.

Chapter Fifteen

HE WASN'T WHERE SHE EXPECTED. HE WAS SITTING, WITH HIS collar turned up and a navy watch cap pulled down around his ears, on a piece of silvered tree trunk, quite close to where she stood. Charlotte recognized the cap—it was his great-uncle's. She thought Oliver might be waiting for her, but she wasn't entirely sure; warily she sat on the log beside him. Neither spoke for a long time. They watched Amos run.

"He needs it." Oliver broke the silence, his voice oddly rough. "He needs to be able to run like that. I wish you liked him better."

"Me?" She was surprised. "I don't mind him. I'm just not crazy about dogs in general—it isn't Amos specially. I can't help it, Oliver. I'm not an animal person."

"Doesn't matter. Let's not sit here, it's too cold."

They walked to where the sand was wet and firm. Amos raced up to them and around them, his big feet throwing up sand and water, then ahead, then back again, and off in a different direction.

"Oliver," said Charlotte at last, "you're right. I don't understand. But I want to, if you'll give me a chance."

He stooped and picked up a pebble, then flung it into the broken waves. "I keep thinking, if only he hadn't died now. If only he was still alive. He *shouldn't* have died, Charlotte—there was no reason for him to. None. Why did he?"

"Because he was old," she said. "Why does anyone die?

134

Unless there's an accident or disease of some kind. I suppose a person just wears out."

But he shook his head. "I'm not talking about a person. I'm talking about my Great-Uncle Sam. *He shouldn't have died.*"

He spoke with such furious passion she stopped and stared at him. His face was no longer carefully composed, his feelings showed with devastating clarity. She was unprepared for the anger. "All this time I've lived with him. I've done everything I could to take care of things, to make life easy for him. The shopping, the cooking, the cleaning. I made sure he took his pills. He didn't have to shovel snow or empty the trash or drive anywhere. That's why I came back from Washington —not because I knew something was going to happen, just to *keep* anything from happening. It isn't fair. It's not *fair*! I only needed a few more years—just to the end of high school. Not very long."

She was shocked. She had known Oliver was feeling something, but she hadn't guessed what it was. A numbness filled her chest. "But, I thought—I mean—you seemed to like him," she said, her voice thin and small.

"What's that got to do with anything? Liking or not liking? Didn't you think he liked me, too? It doesn't make any difference one way or the other now, does it? He's gone anyway and everything's a Godawful mess," he said bitterly. "He made me feel I had a home. He trapped me into believing that it was working out."

"But it was, Oliver."

"I know, that's what I thought. Now what?"

"He didn't die on purpose, to spite you. He probably didn't want to die at all."

"But he did. And I'm worse off than I was before I came to live with him."

"How can you say that? After everything he gave you." She was outraged. It was the ultimate ingratitude. "He had his own life without you—he was getting along fine before you came. I'll bet having you to stay wasn't his idea, but he was willing to share his house with you anyway, and he wasn't—"

"Don't lecture me! You asked me to explain and I'm try-

135

ing. But it isn't what you want to hear, is it? I can't help that, Charlotte, it's the truth. *Listen* to me." He caught her by the arm and swung her to face him. Still holding on, he said fiercely, "He's dead. It's doesn't matter to him, any of this. But I'm alive, and I have to make something out of what's left. He's blown a great hole in my life all of a sudden and I have to figure out what to do, and there isn't any *time*." He gave her a shake. "Can't you understand at all? Can't you?"

She couldn't answer. She didn't know what to say.

He dropped her arm and started walking again, away from her. "Oliver—" But he took no notice. She watched him go and thought of a cold gray afternoon at the beginning of their acquaintance, when by accident she'd come upon him sitting by himself on the hillside overlooking the river. He had told her a little about himself, defiantly, not confidingly. She had escaped from home full of her own troubles, upset and resentful over family changes that seemed certain to ruin her life, and he had given her a glimpse of a life outside her sheltered experience.

It embarrassed her to think what a baby she'd been. Changes were part of being alive, whether she liked them or not—they weren't the end of the world. Her home and family were safely hers, however, no matter what happened: a reliable, secure center. It was different for Oliver, who had been displaced and wandering since his parents divorced each other. He was sent away to school after school because they couldn't or wouldn't cope with him. And then he had landed in Concord, with his great-uncle, and he had stayed. Whatever they had arranged between them seemed to work.

How could he blame the Commodore for dying? She didn't understand that. How could he be so full of bitterness? What should she do? He was getting further away; she felt swamped, desolate. But she didn't want him to go by himself, whether she understood or not.

"Oliver, wait!" She ran after him, caught him up, and thrust her arm under his. She felt the tension in him like electrical current. "Give me a chance, will you? It's just—" She was afraid he wasn't going to respond to her, that he had closed up and shut her out, and she was searching for a way back in to him, when he said, "I did like Uncle Sam, you know. I was really fond of him. But that only makes it worse. You're all right, Charlotte, look what you have. Nobody's ever going to come along and take it all away from you. Even if you lose some of it, there'll be a lot left."

"But you still have a lot left," she protested. "You have friends, and you've got a place to go. I know you don't like your mother very much, but she's *there*. It isn't as if you had nobody and nowhere to go."

"You really don't—yes, she's there. And she'll do her duty because I'm her responsibility and she's run out of alternatives. Even though it won't make either one of us happy." The fury had gone out of him; he still held himself tight, but his voice was level. "I can take care of myself perfectly well. It would solve everything if they'd let me. If I could look after Uncle Sam, I can certainly manage on my own. It wasn't one-sided, you know, our arrangement. He wasn't helpless, like Ophelia, but this last year he really needed—someone to keep an eye on things." He lapsed into silence, brooding. "I have thought about running away, Charlotte. I've thought about it a lot. Just disappearing," he said then.

"You aren't still—?"

"No. It's not practical," he said flatly. "Oh, I could do it—lots of minors do. And it would solve things right now maybe, but there's no future in it. I'm not well enough equipped yet."

"What do you mean, equipped?"

"I don't want to just survive. I want to be able to take care of myself well. And I want to do something interesting with my life, not just get by."

They walked on up the beach, right to the end of the island, without realizing how far they were going. Oliver laced his fingers through Charlotte's and put both their hands into his pocket for warmth. She liked his fingers curled around hers; she was very conscious of him close to her, their shoulders bumping gently, in a way she had never been aware of him before. It distracted her a little from what he was saying. Amos didn't range as far away from them as he had been. His tongue hung like a limp pink ribbon out of the side of his grinning mouth as he lolloped along, swerving now and then to check a particularly intriguing smell. He was blissfully happy.

"No, I'll hang on and work my tail off so I can get into Harvard," Oliver was saying. "Then it won't matter how old I am, it'll be *my* life again. I won't have to answer to anyone else."

"What about your mother? What will she think?"

"Paula?" He gave a humorless little laugh. "She'll be delighted. After all the years she's despaired of me, to find I've settled down. I'll be a credit instead of an embarrassment. And eventually she'll be able to say, 'My son at Harvard,' which is fair enough I suppose since she'll be paying. But she won't have to bother about having me around anymore."

"But, Oliver—what if you don't get into Harvard?" ventured Charlotte. "You sound so sure."

He gave her a sharp look. "I am sure. Don't worry about that. I don't have to count on anyone except myself for that, and I know I can do it."

"You and Andy," she said enviously, "you have your futures all worked out. I wish I had. What am I going to do?"

"You'll go to Radcliffe. Or Wellesley, but it isn't as convenient."

"I will? And who's decided that, if I may ask? I don't even know if I want to go to Wellesley or Radcliffe, Oliver Shattuck, much less that I'd get in if I did. Some of us don't have your confidence."

"Of course you can get in—you aren't dumb. You'd have to work—I told you—but it's worth it for what you want."

"I don't know that it is what I want," she objected. "That's what I'm telling you—I don't know."

His face darkened. "Oh well, you don't have to. You aren't escaping from anything. You don't have to figure out in advance how to make things go the way you want—you can just let them happen and they'll come out right."

"You don't know that."

"Don't be dense, Charlotte. Of course I do. I can tell by looking at the rest of your family. Max and Deb and Eliot. They've all had the chance to try anything they fancied,

138

with a comfortable welcoming place to come back to in between. Why will it be any different for you? Your parents will support you and you know it. Do you have any idea how lucky you are? Last Friday night, for just a little while, I let myself pretend—it was as if—well, it was nice." He ended the sentence abruptly and whistled to Amos. They started back the way they had come.

Charlotte thought of what her mother had said, about Oliver giving his mother a chance. "You know," she began carefully, "it might not be as bad as you expect, living with your mother again. You're older, and a lot has changed."

"Yes, it has," he agreed without joy. "She's a completely different person. She's not really my mother at all anymore. Since the divorce she's moved to Washington, she's gotten herself an important job and a new husband. I wasn't around when any of it was happening. Charlotte, if she'd married Eric in the first place instead of my father, I probably wouldn't exist at all. I doubt she'd have had a child, it's obvious she doesn't need one. For eight years she's managed very nicely without. Now all of a sudden I turn up again and she's stuck. She's obliged to do something about me. Great basis for a relationship, wouldn't you say?"

"But it's what you've got."

"I know that. That's what I've been saying, haven't you been listening?" He stopped, forcing her to stop with him. Her hand was still in his pocket. "Unless . . ."

"Unless what?" She faced him; part of her wanted him to let go, part of her didn't. Her heart had begun to jog, gradually picking up speed.

"You said I had friends."

"You do, Oliver. Of course you do. All of us, the Schuylers, my family—"

"Charlotte," he interrupted. "I need more than friends." Before she had a chance to think, he pulled her tight against him and kissed her fiercely on the mouth. She stood there and let him do it, too surprised to respond. He pulled away and searched her face. She swallowed and heard it thunder in her ears. "Oliver—" Her voice was an odd little squeak. It wasn't the first time he'd kissed her—he'd done it the night after the dance, once they'd taken Kath and Andy home, and before that even, backstage at the Summer Players' production of *The Fantasticks*, when they'd helped Deb with the properties. That had been experimental, playing almost, even though she'd discovered she liked it. This was quite different.

"We aren't just friends," said Oliver and kissed her again. She saw it coming, was prepared, felt it shoot all the way down to her stomach, like warm ginger ale. He meant it, and she kissed him back this time.

"It's all right, isn't it?" he said then.

"Yes, but—no, Oliver, wait. I can't, I mean I didn't expect—"

"Oh, Charlotte!" he exclaimed. "What do you mean, you didn't expect? What *did* you expect?"

Charlotte made a grab for her scattered wits. "It was very sudden. *You* knew what you were going to do, but I didn't. You didn't give me a chance—"

"Look, Charlotte." He shook her gently. "There isn't time. Don't you understand that? It's almost gone."

She looked at him helplessly, afraid of his urgency and touched by it, not knowing what to say that would stall him without making him shut her out. Amos came to her rescue. He clearly thought they had been standing together long enough, whatever they were doing, and needed to be reminded that he was there, too. He pushed his large hairy body between them and panted up at them in an ingratiating manner. Oliver pulled back and let go of Charlotte, and she felt the loss of contact like a shock. To cover it, to give herself a little room, she said the first thing that came into her head: "What time is it, anyway? I'm starving." She was, too. She felt very hollow inside and was relieved to realize there might be a reason for it besides Oliver. She saw his eyes narrow and his face start to go blank. "Oliver," she said calmly, "if you turn around and walk away from me again, I won't speak to you for the rest of the day, I promise you."

His eyes resumed their normal shape and the blankness receded. He merely looked annoyed. She thought she could cope with that.

"I don't remember where we came out onto the beach,"

she said, gazing along it. "It all looks the same."

"No, it doesn't. We came out by the log, back there. We've passed it."

Separate, they retraced their steps and went back into the dunes. Oliver unlocked the car, and Amos leaped immediately into Charlotte's seat, stepping heavily on the bag of pastries. Charlotte pressed her lips together in a thin line and Oliver hauled the dog out again and shoved him, not ungently, into the back while Amos whipped the air with his tail. He kissed Oliver sloppily on the ear and Oliver grunted.

"I'm glad I ate one, anyway," said Charlotte as they drove off. "His claws went through the bag. He can have my share now. They're all mashed."

Oliver found his way back to the center of Newburyport, through the network of unfamiliar streets beside the harbor, to an old block of brick warehouses that had been dressed up and turned into trendy little shops and restaurants. Behind them was a big parking lot only about half full.

"Will he be all right alone in the car?" asked Charlotte as Oliver stopped the car.

"There's a blanket in back for him, and it isn't cold out of the wind."

Amos guessed their intentions and looked woebegone. For a creature with a faceful of hair, Charlotte had to concede that he had an astonishing variety of expressions. Of course, he expressed himself all over, not just with his face: in the way he sat or stood, the angle of his tail and ears, whether he lay with bulky confidence or flattened himself on the floor. "Can I give him one of these?" she asked, knowing how strict Oliver was about food and feeding times. As long as the Commodore had been around, Oliver had had an uphill struggle; Commodore Shattuck was forever palming Amos tidbits or pretending to drop things on the floor. "Don't deprive an old man of his pleasure," the Commodore would say when Oliver caught him at it. "Besides, it's the only way I can get the brute to leave me alone." Oliver just sighed.

"It isn't good for him, that kind of stuff," he said now.

"Or for me either. It's a treat, Oliver."

"Just a piece."

She chose the largest fragment of elephant ear in the bag—an almost whole one. Amos gulped it gratefully in two bites without seeming to chew. His mouth closed wetly around her fingers, but he was very careful not to nip. She wiped her hand hastily on her trousers. They shut him in and left him to make a nest in his navy blanket.

Chapter Sixteen

THERE WAS A SANDWICH SHOP ON THE CORNER, WITH GLASS windows all the way around and a long counter inside where people were eating all sorts of good things, but Oliver walked past it. "If I'm paying, I choose where we go," he said, reading Charlotte's mind.

On up the street was something called the Cafe Florian. The bottom half of its windows were covered with red and white checked curtains, so it was impossible to see inside. The top half of the windows looked very dark to Charlotte. There was a menu posted beside the door. Oliver glanced at it appraisingly, then opened the door for Charlotte. Inside it was small and dim. There were tables covered with red cloths, each with a candle stuck in a wine bottle coated with dripped wax. She was reassured to see other people sitting at some of them, having lunch, even though they were all adults: men in suits and smartly dressed women on their lunch hours. The other place had been like Friendly's, interchangeable with any other sandwich shop, bright and familiar. This was a real restaurant, and though she'd been to many, it had been as a child taken by her parents, not on her own escorted by someone her own age; it made her nervous even as it pleased her. A waitress actually came up to them with menus and showed them to a table. Oliver acted as if he'd done it all dozens of times before, but Charlotte couldn't think when when he would have.

"What would you like?" he said, sounding terribly grown-up, as the waitress stood by. She looked about Deb's age, was wearing black trousers, a slinky white shirt, and a red butcher's apron, which prevented the shirt from being immodest. She kept tucking her limp brown hair behind her ear when it fell across her face. Deb said shoes like hers would ruin your back before you were twenty-eight: they had very high Cuban heels.

Charlotte guessed that Oliver would not like it if she asked about prices and whether or not he could afford what she most wanted. If he couldn't, he shouldn't have brought her in, and she decided she deserved and needed a good lunch. The warmth of the cafe was making her realize exactly how tired and hungry she was. She ordered spaghetti with clam sauce, French bread, and because the waitress had reminded her of Deb, a spinach salad. Evidently the exercise and emotional turmoil of the morning had given Oliver an appetite as well, for he ordered broiled fish, baked potato, and coleslaw. The waitress gave him a calculating look, but wrote it all down and disappeared.

As if by agreement, they hardly spoke until the food had come and they had taken the edge off their hunger. When he'd eaten his fish and half of his potato, Oliver said, "Look, Charlotte," and she braced herself. They hadn't resolved anything on the beach, she was aware of that, but she'd allowed herself to hope that he would let it rest. At least there were other people around them now; they would have to be careful. "We have to talk."

She took a deep breath and let it out slowly. "All right."

"I've known you for almost three years. That's a long time, about as long as I've known anyone. Do you feel the way I do?"

"I don't know, Oliver. I'm—I'm not sure how you feel."

"I thought I made it very clear. What more do you want? We wouldn't be here if I didn't feel strongly, you ought to know that. And you shouldn't have come if you didn't."

It was useless to protest that she hadn't realized what she was getting herself into when she'd stayed in the car instead of going to school. And would it be true? She looked at Oliver and knew suddenly how badly she was going to miss him, but what did that mean? She had to be able to work it out, and he was pushing her.

"I need to be sure of you," he said in a low voice.

"But aren't you sure?"

"No."

"Well, then what have we been doing for the past three years? I thought we were friends, good friends. All four of us."

"Look around," said Oliver, an edge in his voice. "We aren't all here, are we? I told you before, Charlotte, I'm not talking about friends. Don't pretend you don't know what I mean. What do you think goes on among the other kids at school? They aren't playing hopscotch anymore, you know. They're getting serious about each other. They're pairing off and going on dates, making commitments to each other."

"Not all of them," said Charlotte.

"No," agreed Oliver. "The ones who love each other."

She couldn't look at him. She watched her fingers destroying a piece of French bread. "What about Andy and Kath?" she asked finally.

"What about them?"

"It changes everything. I mean, if we—if—"

"It's been bound to happen anyway," he said briskly. "Sooner or later. Now it's sooner. We couldn't go on and on that way, the four of us. It doesn't mean we can't be friends still."

But she thought of Kath, too desperate to hide her feelings, and of Andy, his cold hand gripping hers by the woodpile, trying so hard to tell her what he believed. "It won't be the same."

"Is that all you want? To have it forever be the same?"

"Oh, I don't know, Oliver. It's just—" She stopped, then began again. "For years and years my best friend was Eliot. I didn't really have any others. We did all kinds of things together and it was wonderful."

"I know," said Oliver. "You've told me. Often."

She ignored his tone of voice. "I thought it was the end of the world when he announced he was leaving. But the thing was that as long as Eliot was around I didn't feel as if I *needed* any other friends. It's different growing up in my kind of family, where everyone's years and years older. In some ways you get treated like the baby, because you are, and in some ways you get treated like an adult, because everyone else is."

"It's better than having no family."

"I don't mind," said Charlotte. "I'm not complaining about it. But when Eliot left me and I thought I wouldn't have anyone—" She gave a little shrug. "—there were the three of you, and we got to be friends. Sometimes in spite of each other," she added with a little smile. "It's been special, for me anyway. I know things change. I don't like it, but I know it happens. It's just that—just that I'm not ready yet."

"Maybe I'm not either," said Oliver. "But that's irrelevant now. Somebody dropped a bomb on me. I'm doing the best I can, but I can't—I have to know about you."

"Why now? Everything isn't coming to an end," she protested. "Why does it have to be this minute, today?"

"Shhh," he hissed, glancing around.

"Would you like something for dessert?" The waitress was back, looking bored.

At the beginning, Charlotte had been going to ask for a chocolate cream puff with ice cream, which, according to her habit of reading menus backward, she had already picked out. But she no longer felt like it. The spaghetti was sitting in a hard lump in her stomach.

"Coffee, please," said Oliver brusquely.

Charlotte shook her head miserably.

"One coffee." The waitress clattered their dishes away.

"Well," said Oliver coldly, "shall we be penpals, then? You can write and tell me all about when Andy asks you out."

"When Andy—?"

"Of course he will. Don't be so thick, Charlotte. You'll be here and I'll be thousands of miles away. What chance have I got then?"

"Will that be all?"

"Yes," he said, distracted.

The waitress scribbled figures on her pad, ripped off the

146

sheet, and put it face down on the table by Oliver's place. "Pay at the desk, please," she said and left them.

"What do you mean, thousands of miles away?" demanded Charlotte when she'd gone. "Washington isn't—"

"I won't *be* in Washington." He stirred his coffee so violently it spilled into the saucer.

She waited.

"It's Eric," he said finally. "He's going on assignment to London. I found out at Christmas, but I didn't think it would make any difference to me then." He gave a bitter little smile. "Paula was all upset because it means leaving her job."

"How long?" asked Charotte in a whisper.

"At least a year, maybe longer."

"A year? But then—you can't—you won't be here this summer."

"That's right. Now do you see?"

"Do you have to go with them? I mean, there are boarding schools—you've been to boarding school before."

"It won't do this time. Paula isn't going to send me away. It's too complicated."

"But we should be able to do *some*thing."

"You can. I've told you what you can do. Charlotte, why won't you? I'm not asking you to go to bed with me, for God's sake. I just want you to say you love me and you'll wait until I can get back."

"I will. I'll be here."

He studied her face, his eyes intent, his jaw tight. "It's no good, is it."

"You're pushing so hard, Oliver. It's not fair."

"What's fair? Uncle Sam dying? My having to leave Concord? Having to go live with two people who don't really want me, but who are going to make me do it anyway? What about me, Charlotte? What have I got? I won't even have Amos."

"Amos? What do you mean?"

"Exactly what I said," he declared bitterly. "You don't think I can take him with me, do you?"

"But he's yours."

"Oh, Charlotte. I couldn't take him even if I were going

147

to Washington—there's no room for him in a city apartment with no yard. But I'm going to London. Dogs have to be quarantined for *six months* over there. Shut up in some kennel. There isn't any way he could go."

"But what will you do?" she asked, shocked.

He picked up the bill and examined it carefully, his mouth set in a tight, grim line.

"Oliver—"

"I'm going to take him to the animal hospital. Wednesday morning."

"They'll find him a home?"

"No."

There was an awful silence; Charlotte stared at him. "You can't—you can't do that," she protested feebly.

"He's mine. You said it yourself."

"But that's not—I didn't mean—how *can* you?"

"I really don't see that there's any choice," he said in a flat voice. "I love him very much, Charlotte. I don't know anyone who would love him as much as I do. There isn't time for me to find him a home myself, and I can't take a chance on someone else doing it. I've made up my mind. Dr. Russell knows. It doesn't hurt. I don't want to talk about it anymore."

There was nothing she could say anyway; he had withdrawn from her. Thoroughly shaken, devastated, she followed him out into the bright windy afternoon. They walked along the street, pretending to look in shop windows, not speaking, cut apart from each other. Charlotte was overwhelmed with a sense of failure, and resentful. Oliver had no right to do that to her. His desperate intensity frightened her. The harder he pressed, the more she wanted to retreat. But London. It was a whole ocean away, another country, unimaginable. As far away as California. She remembered what she'd said to Kath about that. For an instant she wondered what it would do to Kath when she found out, but she was too full of her own problems to spare Kath more than a fleeting thought. And Amos—she shied away from that altogether; she couldn't imagine it. How could Oliver even contemplate . . .

He stopped at a delicatessen and bought a package of very expensive bologna for Amos, and Charlotte suddenly thought about home. "What time is it?" she asked the cashier.

It was quarter of three.

"What does it matter?" said Oliver.

"We should have been home from school by now," said Charlotte in horror. "Mom was leaving work early to be there when your mother comes. They'll wonder—nobody knows where we are."

"It's too late now."

"They'll be furious."

"So?"

"I'll have to call. I'll have to find a pay phone."

He stood outside the booth, with his hands in his pockets, detached, impatient, while she telephoned. She didn't know what it would cost, so she rang the operator to make it collect, and at the last moment, instead of her own number, she gave Deb's.

"Charlotte? What the hell, if you'll pardon me, are you doing in Newburyport?" demanded her sister as soon as she'd accepted the charges. Deb's voice carried very clearly across the wires. "Mother called fifteen minutes ago to ask if I'd seen you. She sounded extremely annoyed, I can tell you. *Newburyport?* How did you get there? Then you haven't been to school today at all. And you didn't tell anyone you were taking off? Do you know how dumb that is?"

"It's very complicated."

"Are you all right? Nothing's happened? You haven't had an accident?"

"No. Oliver—we just wanted to get away. What about Oliver's mother—do you know when she'll get there?"

"I expect she'll be waiting for you at the front door," said Deb dryly. "They left earlier than they'd planned."

They were being cornered. "Oh hell," said Charlotte bleakly.

"Look, Charlotte, I don't know what you've been doing up there or why you went, but you'd better start back as soon as you put the receiver down."

"Will you call Mom?"

149

"Why do I always get stuck in the middle of other people's messes?" grumbled Deb.

"Yes, but will you?"

She must have heard the desperation in Charlotte's voice, because she said in quite another tone, "*Is* everything all right? What about Oliver?"

Charlotte glanced at him, but he'd turned his back. "I don't know. It's just—I wish—"

"Listen, kid, there's no point in getting tangled up in it now, on the phone," said Deb sensibly. "Wait until you aren't running up my phone bill and we can talk about things more easily. Okay? Just get him in the car and point him toward Concord. I'll do what I can with Mother. It might not be too bad, actually. We're all having dinner at the Inn, everyone will be on good behavior."

"Thanks, Deb."

"And for heaven's sake, drive carefully, even if it makes you later. The traffic on 128 will be fearful."

"Yes, we will."

"Well," said Oliver when she came out. "That made everything all right, did it?"

"I called Deb," returned Charlotte shortly. "Your mother will be in Concord before we are."

"That should be jolly. We ought to get a warm welcome, then."

"It's going to be awful."

"You get used to it," said Oliver.

Before they started back, however, Oliver gave Amos the bologna, which he wolfed, and walked him around the parking lot. With great absorption, Amos studied the invisible signs left by local dogs on tree trunks, curbstones, and parking meter poles, then covered them with his own. Charlotte watched with distaste.

Oliver had some trouble finding his way out of the town, but after a glance at his face, Charlotte declined to offer any advice, even though if she had, it would have speeded the process. Actually, the whole trip home was nasty. About twenty minutes after they'd gotten onto Interstate 95 Amos began to make peculiar wheezing noises through his whiskers. They got louder and louder—a sort of rasping, choking sound —and just as Charlotte, alarmed, opened her mouth to ask Oliver what was wrong, Amos was vigorously sick all over the back seat. At the sight and the smell, Charlotte went pale, and her own stomach gave an ominous lurch. There was nothing Oliver could do when it happened: he had a car practically against his rear bumper, several alongside in the fast lane, and nowhere to get safely off the highway.

"Roll down your window, will you?" he exclaimed impatiently.

Charlotte did, and hung out of it, breathing great draughts of cold air and willing her lunch to stay put. Amos thrust his muzzle out beside her ear; his ears blew madly. She did her best to ignore him. By the time Oliver found a rest area, she thought she was fairly steady. Oliver put Amos on his leash and handed him to her to get him out of the way. Now that he'd rid himself of what had upset him, Amos was quite recovered and eager to explore. He dragged Charlotte about enthusiastically.

Oliver was left to clean up. It was obvious that Charlotte would have been a far greater liability than help, but it didn't improve Oliver's mood, nor did the fact that what Amos had thrown up was the bologna. It was still quite recognizable; there was no sign of the pastry.

Underway again, they had to drive with the window open. Oliver had done as well as he could without adequate supplies, but a strong sweet-sour smell clung to the back seat.

At the Route 128 interchange, all of a sudden the traffic caught them. Cars clogged the road, so close together they seemed to be coupled like a train, moving at a terrifying speed. Those that were going even faster whipped in and out of lanes without warning. Once Oliver got them into the flow, he had no choice but to go fast himself.

Unconsciously, Charlotte pushed her feet hard against the rise of the floor in front and her back against the seat. Oliver hunched forward over the steering wheel, his face tight, his eyes flicking constantly to the rearview mirror. It was far worse than it had been that morning; now everyone was going home and frantic to get there. Trapped in the furious rush, the Commodore's little Ford hurtled along helplessly, until at last Oliver said, without shifting his eyes, "I can't do this much longer. We have to get out. Look at the map and see what else we can do."

Charlotte unclenched herself with difficulty—every muscle in her body was taut—and found the map. "But I don't know where we are."

"Route Sixty-two. Look for Route Sixty-two and see if it's anything we can take. Quick, will you? We're almost there."

By the time she had found the road they were on, they had reached the vital exit, and in desperation, Oliver had taken it. The difference was immediate. Even if they were lost, it was worth it to have broken free of the torrent of cars. He pulled into a gas station, took the map from her, and studied it. Gradually Charlotte's pulse and respiration slowed, and her body eased. "Can we?" she asked.

He gave a brief nod. "You'll have to watch—we stay on this all the way to Bedford. It won't be as fast."

"Thank heaven!" she said fervently.

But Oliver looked grim; he didn't like being defeated by a road, she guessed, on top of everything else. They hardly said two words the rest of the way back to Concord. Oliver's silence was remote, and Charlotte's more and more depressed.

Chapter Seventeen

IT WAS A QUARTER OF FIVE BY THE TIME THEY PULLED INTO the Paiges' driveway, and Charlotte was feeling utterly miserable. She sat immobile in the car after Oliver stopped it, staring out the window blankly. They had worked nothing out between them, and now it was too late. From now on there would be other people around, the web of details surrounding the Commodore's service and Oliver's future snaring them hopelessly.

"Oliver—"

"We'd better go in," he said brusquely. "It's pointless to sit here."

And he did, and she had to follow. Deb met them at the back door; she looked at them appraisingly, first Oliver, then Charlotte, and frowned a little, but what she said was, "You're in luck. The Prestons have gone to the Inn, and Dad isn't home yet. So it's just Mother you've got to face right now. If you're smart, you'll take my advice and crawl a little. Be apologetic. And for heaven's sake, don't answer back."

"Do the Prestons know that we've been gone?" asked Charlotte, hoping.

"Oh yes. They've been here already looking for Oliver; and they're coming back for drinks in about an hour. If you were a couple of years older I'd give you each a good stiff one right now—you look as if you could use it. What took you so long?"

"Oh," said Charlotte, "it was—"

"Several things," cut in Oliver. "Nothing important."

"Mmmp," said Deb. "Let me take Amos. Go and tell Mother you're back."

Mrs. Paige was in the living room running the vacuum cleaner over carpet that Charlotte had seen her vacuum thoroughly the day before. She stopped when they appeared in the doorway and regarded them unsmilingly. "So you're back," she said. "I was beginning to wonder if we'd ever see you again. I didn't expect this of either of you, I must say. I thought you had more sense than to go off like that without telling anyone. If something had happened we wouldn't have had any idea where you were."

"But nothing did," said Oliver.

"I'm sorry, Mom," said Charlotte quickly, seeing the steely expression on her mother's face. "I truly am. It's—we didn't think."

"No, I guess you didn't," agreed Mrs. Paige. "Charlotte, that's not like you. Why on earth would you do such a thing?"

"I thought we needed some time," said Oliver. He was very cool and self-possessed, not at all apologetic. "We weren't going to get it any other way. If we'd told you, you wouldn't have let us go."

Charlotte winced inwardly. He was doing it all wrong, she knew even without watching her mother. Why couldn't he have listened to Deb?

"You're quite right," said Mrs. Paige in a cold, clipped voice. "And we would have had very good reasons, Oliver. For you to have done it by yourself, while you were here as our responsibility is bad enough, but for Charlotte to have gone as well—" She stopped abruptly. "I'm not going to go into this any further with you right now. You had better go upstairs and wash and change. You weren't here when the Prestons arrived, you'd better be here when they come back. Charlotte, I put your red dress out."

"Why did you do that?" whispered Charlotte fiercely to Oliver as they went up. "You only made it worse."

But he ignored her and went down the hall to Eliot's room, at the far end, and closed the door behind him.

154

What Charlotte actually wanted to do more than anything else was throw herself face down on her bed and dissolve in angry, hurt, self-pitying tears. To let all the confused, contradictory feelings flood out into her pillow and to have someone come and comfort her and tell her everything was all right and could be fixed, put back in order again, and she needn't worry anymore. But her red jersey dress was spread neatly on the bed, and she knew no one was going to come. Her mother was upset and cross, and Oliver had closed off communications because she hadn't said the right things when he wanted her to, and his mother and stepfather would be there in less than an hour, further complicating everything. If only . . . if only what? She was suddenly too tired to think.

"Buck up," said Deb. "There's no point in looking tragic, it'll only remind everyone. Best thing is to take their minds off it. The rules of civilized behavior say that people do not chew their children out in front of other people, so if you play your cards right, by the end of the evening they'll have calmed down."

"You think so?" said Charlotte without much hope. She had made herself reasonably presentable and gone down the back stairs, finding her own company too depressing to keep any longer. "You didn't hear Oliver talking to Mom. He did just what you said not to."

"He would. Had you two been planning this?"

"No. At least I hadn't."

"It wasn't very bright, you know. Not the best way to win sympathy and influence people."

"I honestly didn't think about—about this part of it till just before I called you. He offered to let me out at school this morning. I didn't *have* to go . . ."

"But?"

"But then he'd have gone alone."

Deb stopped cutting carrot sticks and turned to Charlotte. "And you couldn't let him do that," she said.

"I couldn't."

Deb's eyes softened with sympathy. "Did you get any-where?"

"Oh, Deb," said Charlotte unhappily. "It's such a mess."

They heard the front door bell. Deb's face clouded. "Hell," she said succinctly. "Here, you finish this while I let them in. Concentrate hard on not cutting yourself. It'll help." She gave Charlotte's shoulder a quick squeeze, then added, "And don't let them see anything's wrong."

Deb was right about the rules: all the adults understood and played by them. The only mention of Charlotte and Oliver's misbehavior was an oblique one made by Paula as she greeted her son. She gave him a quick kiss on the cheek and said pointedly how sorry she and Eric had been, after going to considerable trouble to arrange a few extra hours that afternoon to see the lawyer, to find Oliver not there when they arrived. Oliver said nothing, and Mr. Paige looked faintly questioning—he still knew nothing about any of it—but the moment passed into introductions. They had none of them met Oliver's stepfather before.

Eric Preston was not as tall as Charlotte had expected from seeing him on television, and he looked older; there was quite a lot of gray in his dark hair and little lines at the corners of his eyes that didn't show on camera. He had a well-defined, confident face, pleasant and interested. There was something about his eyes, however, that reminded Charlotte forcibly of Oliver, something that made her wonder what he was thinking as he smiled and shook hands. They made a very attractive pair, Paula and Eric. She found it hard to think of them as Mr. and Mrs. Preston, however. As long as she had known him, Oliver had referred to his mother as Paula, and Eric was always Eric Preston on television.

Everyone made polite general conversation as they settled themselves around the living room: about the flight from Washington and how bad the traffic out of Boston was, the amount of snow on the ground and the severity of the winter. No one mentioned Commodore Shattuck, or the reason they were together, or the memorial service the next day. If Charlotte had not known better, she would have thought it was an ordinary cocktail party. Her sense of unreality was so great that for an instant she actually wondered if the whole thing

156

weren't some bizarre mistake, but a glance at Oliver and she knew it wasn't.

He passed the drinks as Mr. Paige made them, and Charlotte, to have something to do, passed nuts and raw vegetables and dip, earning a look of approval from her mother. Oliver was remote and handsome in a dark blue blazer and gray flannel slacks. But Charlotte experienced an odd and uncomfortable sensation at the sight of him, a kind of numbing shyness she hadn't encountered in their relationship before. She avoided contact of any sort with him. He seemed unaware.

"What about Ronald Reagan then?" Deb dropped the question into a brief lull. She had lodged herself on a straight-backed chair next to Eric Preston. "What do you think his chances are? Could he really do it?"

Eric Preston sat comfortably back in the green wing chair, listening to her questions, smiling a little, taking time to choose his answers. It was strange to see him sitting there in three dimensions, Charlotte reflected, instead of flat on the television screen, but it was just added to the feeling of dislocation that was fogging her head.

On the pretext of getting more ice, Mrs. Paige went over to Mr. Paige, and Charlotte heard her say in an undertone, "I didn't think to warn him about Deb. Gordon, perhaps you should—"

"I expect he can take care of himself, Kit. He must have to cope with Debs all the time."

Mrs. Paige did not look convinced. "Well, we'll have to separate them at dinner, I think." She sat on the couch with Paula, who asked about Hilary. They were such a contrast together: her mother crisp and tailored in gray wool that complemented her short gray hair; Paula almost young enough to be her daughter, fair-skinned and honey-blonde in a soft geranium-colored dress. Mrs. Paige was straight neat lines and Paula curving fluid ones.

"I don't feel a bit like a grandmother," said Mrs. Paige, "at least not until I've spent a couple of hours with Hilary. She's a darling, but I'm so glad she's Jean's baby, not mine."

Paula smiled. "They're such a lot of work. Is Jean staying home with her?"

"Until she's ready for nursery school."

"I admire women who choose to stay home," replied Paula a little too firmly. "Of course I had to work—Alan was in graduate school and we were desperate for the money. But it was a good thing—I'm sure I would have gone crazy otherwise. I'm simply not the domestic type."

"I didn't mind while the children were young. I did a lot of volunteer work during those years, but I was quite happy raising a family. Things have changed so much—"

"Vermouth," said Mr. Paige, distracting Charlotte. He put a glass in her hand, which held a lot of ice and a little pale yellow liquid. It tasted very faintly of varnish; she wondered how much of it she would have to drink in order for it to untie the knots inside her. She had no idea, but she didn't think people usually got tight on vermouth. "Was school all right?"

Her father was frowing at her, and she realized he'd asked the question twice. She held her second sip a moment before swallowing it. "Well, actually—" Out of the corner of her eye she saw Oliver standing by the bookcases, swirling the cubes in his own glass around and around. "Actually—"

Mr. Paige lifted his eyebrows inquiringly.

"Well, we didn't actually go."

The eyebrows flickered. "You didn't? But this morning, I thought that was the plan. Wasn't it?"

She let out her breath. "It was, but it—changed. You see—"

"This have to do with Oliver not being here this afternoon?"

Charlotte nodded. Mr. Paige looked at her assessingly, but kept to the rules. "You can explain it to me later. Now, who needs to be refreshed? Paula, can I get you some more?"

Conversation scattered briefly, like a flock of birds disturbed, then resettled, and Charlotte drifted over to sit by the hearth. There was no fire that evening because they were going out, and no one had thought to build one anyway. The last log Oliver had put on Friday lay across the andirons only partially burned.

Mr. Paige deftly inserted himself between Deb and Eric and began to tell an involved story about a New York art dealer caught selling forgeries. After her initial irritation wore off, Deb allowed herself to enjoy it.

"Oliver," said Paula suddenly, "come and sit down. I feel as if you're lurking back there."

With the briefest hesitation he did as she asked, and she went on talking to Mrs. Paige without looking at him. He sat neatly on his chair, still watching the ice in his glass, physically present, somewhere else mentally, Charlotte was certain. She had come to know that closed expression very well. Paula didn't seem to notice.

They had gotten onto the subject of London, and it was obvious from Mrs. Paige's comments that this was not the first she'd heard of the trip.

"Now of course we've had to change our plans entirely," Paula was saying. "Originally Eric was going at the beginning of next month by himself and I was going to stay in Washington for another eight or nine weeks to finish a couple of projects. But that simply isn't practical under the circumstances. We have to find a school for Oliver, and the sooner we get settled the better. But there's so much to do and so little time. I've got two grants in crucial stages and no one else knows enough about them."

"What about a place to live?" asked Mrs. Paige. "Do they find you one or are you on your own?"

Paula gave her head a little shake. "That's another problem. "We've been promised a flat in Hampstead in April—Eric was going to be in a hotel until I arrived, which would have been fine. But that's not possible now—we must have a place of our own right away. It's very awkward."

"I'm sure it will work out," said Mrs. Paige.

"Oh, I suppose it will," agreed Paula with a sigh. "I would have arranged things completely differently if I'd thought that—" She didn't look at Oliver, but Charlotte could see her become suddenly aware of him, although he hadn't moved or spoken. She smiled determinedly. "Of course it will. And it'll be a marvelous experience for Oliver—the chance to live in another country. The school system will be different—"

"He's been doing very well here," said Mrs. Paige, and Charlotte was grateful to her.

159

"Yes, I know he has. We've seen his reports. That should make it easier."

Charlotte wondered if they had tennis teams in English schools, and if Oliver would have to wear a uniform. Without realizing it she had been staring at Paula; she discovered that Paula was staring back at her, a curious unreadable expression on her face, as if she were trying to see what Charlotte was thinking. Charlotte went hot with embarrassment and got up quickly to offer around the dry-roasted peanuts.

"What time is our reservation, Eric?" asked Paula. "We thought early because tomorrow will be hectic."

"It's nice of you to include us all," said Mr. Paige.

"It's the very least we could do after everything you've done for us," she replied. "I don't know how we'd manage without you. Oliver's father is on his way to some sort of conference in San Antonio—said he couldn't possibly change his plans at the last minute. I barely caught him before he left. Not that I expected him to come. He said he was sure we could handle everything." There was a definite chill in her voice.

"And so, with your generous help, we can," said Eric equably. "You've been specially good to Oliver."

"Well, of course. He's almost one of the family," said Mr. Paige. "Now, what about coats?"

"I'll get them," said Oliver without prompting.

Charlotte and Oliver rode with the Prestons, in the back seat of their plush-upholstered rented Buick. "You go with them," said Mrs. Paige quietly to Charlotte, and Charlotte couldn't very well say she'd rather not, so she nodded. "Are you feeling all right?" asked Mrs. Paige, giving her a second look. She nodded again, and then Eric was helping her mother on with her coat.

It was a short drive. Oliver sat behind Eric, his face to the window. Charlotte, on her side of the car, was painfully conscious of him; part of her ached to reach across and touch him, put her hand on his, but she couldn't. He was too far away.

"I don't know this part of the country," remarked Eric conversationally. "It looks just as advertised: old graveyards, colonial houses, white churches, lots of snow. We had a chance to drive around a bit this afternoon. Saw people out skating. Do you skate?"

There was a moment's silence, then Charlotte plunged in to fill it. "Yes, we do. Some friends of ours have their own pond. It's not very big, of course," she added in case he got the wrong idea. "Sometimes we go to Punkatasset or Walden, and usually the river freezes for a week or two at least."

Paula turned her head slightly. "You don't actually skate on the river, do you? I'd have thought it was awfully deep, and the currents—"

"Walden Pond," said Eric. "Good lord, I remember struggling with Thoreau when I was a freshman in college. About all I can remember of *Walden* is 'The mass of men lead lives of quiet desperation.' Our professor used to quote it at us all the time with a kind of wild expression in his eyes. Tell me, Charlotte, is there really a hut?"

"There used to be. Now there's only a cairn—a mound of stones, where it stood. People bring them from all over to add to it. And there's a trail around the pond. In the summer there are too many people though, it's not very nice. They come to swim."

"There's more open land here than I expected," Eric went on. He was talking directly to Charlotte, glancing at her in the rearview mirror. "I thought it would be nothing but suburbs."

"There are quite a few farms still, like the one where we work summers. And lots of conservation land. Commodore Shattuck was on the Conservation Commission," she said, almost defiantly. It was the first time anyone had mentioned his name that evening. She wondered if she was breaking one of the rules.

But Eric said easily, "I'm originally from Florida myself. They could use more people concerned with conservation down there, I can tell you. It's been developed out of recognition—hotels, shopping malls, condominiums. I hate to go back. Once the land's gone you never have another chance. Even though I'm a city person, it's nice to know there's some country left."

161

The dining room at the Inn was warm and golden, comfortable with the murmur of well-modulated voices and the clink of silver on china. They sat at a large round table with pink and white carnations in the middle, and Mrs. Paige unobtrusively maneuvered Deb away from Eric. From the glint in her eye, Charlotte guessed that Deb knew precisely what her mother was doing and why, but she made no comment.

It wasn't the occasion for arguing. The rules of civilized behavior dictated what they should talk about and how they should respond to one another. Charlotte couldn't decide whether it was evasion, or a way of dealing with the underlying situation; whichever, the adults carried it off with skill. For herself, she was finding it increasingly difficult to operate on two levels. She had begun to get a headache with the first course, which didn't help. Every now and then she caught Deb looking at her with a faintly concerned expression and hastily averted her eyes. Her balance was precarious enough without Deb's sympathy to upset it altogether. She concentrated fiercely on what was being said, and afterward couldn't remember any of it, just Oliver sitting across from her like someone she barely knew.

Chapter Eighteen

CHARLOTTE WALKED TO SCHOOL THE NEXT MORNING ALONE. IT was a cold, grim day: the sun was smothered in heavy layers of cloud, the air so sharp it felt like breathing splinters. January at its most uncompromising. The world was locked in bitter gray light, and cars drove to work with their parking lights on. Charlotte huddled inside her clothes, burdened with Oliver's books as well as her own, and felt as grim as the day. She was edgy and tired and apprehensive about school. The alternative, staying home, was as bad or worse, she decided during the night.

So she simply got up and dressed for school, collected her things, ate breakfast, and left the house at the usual time, all without discussion. She had hardly slept, in spite of the long, exhausting day; her brain refused to stop working. She lay tense in the darkness hour after hour thinking and thinking and getting hopelessly snarled. The longing she'd felt earlier, for someone to comfort her, talk to her, understand, solve everything, came back more fiercely. But no one could do for her what she wanted: assure her beyond doubt that things would work out between Oliver and Paula and Eric, or convince him that he was wrong about Amos. No one could tell her how she felt about Oliver, or what she should do herself. The realization of how alone she was had grown coldly inside her when her mother had come in to talk while Charlotte was getting ready for bed. Mrs. Paige was quiet and serious, but her face was no longer full of sharp, angry lines.

163

"Darling, you do understand why I was so upset with you when you came home," she said, sitting on the bed. "You mustn't think I'm unsympathetic—I know this is a hard time."

Charlotte made a thorough job of hanging up her clothes.

"I couldn't imagine where you were this afternoon. When Paula and Eric arrived early and I couldn't tell them where Oliver was or when he'd be back, I felt simply awful."

"But it wasn't your fault. She didn't blame you, did she?" said Charlotte.

"As long as Oliver's under our roof, he's our responsibility. I wasn't happy about letting him take the car this morning, neither was your father, but we trusted him to do what he said he would. I suppose it was too great a temptation, and we should simply have said no."

"But it was all right—nothing happened." She heard herself echoing Oliver's words.

"That's not the point, Charlotte. You're lucky, both of you, that nothing *did* happen, but that's a whole different matter. You knew the situation—you knew the Prestons were coming and that there was a lot to do. We all have a great deal on our minds right now. But for you two to drive off like that, without telling anyone, let alone asking permission— I honestly expected you to have more consideration than that, darling. You're old enough to think of other people."

"But I did," protested Charlotte. "That's why I went. I was thinking of Oliver."

Her mother gave her a long, penetrating look. "Did you know he was planning to do that?"

"Not exactly, but—"

Mrs. Paige sighed. "It *is* my fault, at least partly. I ought to have guessed that something like this was bound to happen. He's been unnaturally stoic from the beginning. He hardly opened his mouth this evening."

"Neither did I," Charlotte pointed out.

"Do you want to talk about what you did all day?" asked her mother with genuine concern. "I might be able to help."

"We walked on the beach, then we had lunch in a restaurant, and we talked. I called Deb, and we came home." Something in Mrs. Paige's voice and face made Charlotte cautious.

164

"What did you talk about?"

She gave a little shrug. "About Commodore Shattuck and Oliver moving away—he told me about going to London. Things like that."

"I'm not trying to pry, darling. But I'm afraid Oliver's much more disturbed about all this than he seems. He could get himself into serious trouble. If there's something we can do—"

"He won't do anything like that again, if that's what you mean. He said he won't."

Mrs. Paige continued to look at her, as if trying to guess what Charlotte wasn't saying. "I know Oliver's your friend, and I know how much you've helped him. But you mustn't—sometimes, Charlotte, you can do someone harm by trying to protect him. This is an awful lot for you to handle. You mustn't let yourself think you have to do it alone. We all want to help, your father and I as well as Paula and Eric."

The temptation was almost overwhelming: her mother was so close, so loving, so ready to listen. But if Charlotte tried stumblingly to tell her about Oliver, what would she hear? To Mrs. Paige they were still both children, and Charlotte was *her* child; she was not impartial. Charlotte had never wanted her to be. But instinctively Charlotte realized that if she talked to her mother about those things she most wanted to, she would be risking her mother's sympathy for Oliver. And she couldn't do that—it was already fragile. All she could do was shake her head miserably and say, "I know."

"Do you feel all right?" asked her mother gently.

Charlotte took a shaky breath. "I'm very tired. It's been an awfully long day and my head aches."

Mrs. Paige put a hand against her cheek. "No fever." She smiled reassuringly and gathered Charlotte into her arms and hugged her. Charlotte rested her head on her mother's shoulder and wondered why life had to be so complicated.

School was every bit as bad as she had expected it to be. The sense of isolation was strong in her, intensified by the familiar surge and clatter. All around her people were doing what they normally did: talking, laughing, shoving each

165

other, touching. It was as if they were speaking a language she couldn't decipher any more.

Her teachers were very understanding about the work she'd have to catch up with; she had no awkward explaining to do, they all seemed to know. All except for Mr. Gerrold, who evidently hadn't noticed that she'd been absent from two algebra classes and gave her the same quiz he gave everyone else. He neither knew, nor particularly seemed to care, why she wasn't prepared, and merely said when she went up to see him at the end of class that if she got a D he'd see about giving her another quiz later.

But the worst of school, as she'd known it would be, was seeing Andy and Kath. The main reason she stayed back to talk to Mr. Gerrold wasn't her grade; she was trying to avoid Kath, who shared algebra and next period French with her and usually walked with her from one to the other. Charlotte hoped in vain that Kath wouldn't wait.

She was there, right outside the door, however. "You weren't in school yesterday. I thought you would be."

Charlotte mumbled vaguely about there being a lot to do.

"Is his mother here?"

"She came yesterday." Charlotte walked as fast as she could through the clogged halls. "We'll be late for class."

Kath wrapped her arms around her books and hugged them tight against her chest, her chin on the edge of her notebook. "How long is she going to stay?"

"They're leaving tomorrow at noon," said Charlotte abruptly. "Hurry up, Kath." Little as she wanted to prolong the conversation, Charlotte couldn't simply detach herself. Even in the midst of her own personal fog, she could sense Kath's desperation.

"Tomorrow? Oliver—is Oliver going, too?"

Desperate herself, Charlotte snapped, "Of course he's going. What else would he do? You didn't seriously think he could stay here by himself, did you?"

"But there's *us*. He's not by himself. I told you. I bet you didn't even try, did you?"

"*Kath*—"

The bell rang. Charlotte spun away from Kath's accusing

166

face, eeled through the classroom door and sank into her seat. Kath followed a moment later, her jaw set, her cheeks blotchy. Charlotte opened her book and refused to look at Kath again. The only way was to be angry with her: for showing her feelings so blatantly, for being so awkward and caring so much and letting Charlotte see that she did. Charlotte had more than enough to deal with herself; she didn't need Kath's wretchedness.

Kath made no further attempt to talk to her during school. As if by prior agreement, they separated for lunch, Kath going off to join some of her basketball teammates. Charlotte glanced around the cafeteria and saw Lynn Cunningham and Bonnie Trincaro beckoning to her. They smiled a little hesitantly at her as she sat down, and Bonnie said, "Um, we're really sorry, Charlotte. About—well, about Commodore Shattuck."

Lynn nodded earnestly.

"It was really unexpected, wasn't it? I mean, he wasn't sick or anything."

"No."

Lynn and Bonnie exchanged a glance, and Lynn said, "What about Oliver? Didn't he find him? God, I can't imagine it. I'd fall apart if it was me."

"Well, he didn't."

There was an uncomfortable silence. Charlotte wished she'd chosen a table by herself. It wasn't Lynn and Bonnie—*she* was the one hopelessly dislocated. She couldn't explain to them, and furthermore, she didn't want to try. That was a big part of the problem, she realized: she couldn't face going back to the beginning, wherever that was, to tell people who didn't know; she was too involved with what was happening *now*.

"The service is this afternoon?" Lynn was saying.

Charlotte merely nodded and ate her potato salad. It stuck in a lump in her throat.

They gave up then, not knowing what else to say, and began to discuss February vacation. They had both signed up for the ski trip to Waterville Valley.

The only skiing Charlotte had ever done was cross-country,

on trails in Concord. She and Oliver had both been given skis two Christmases ago, in time for the great blizzard, when roads across the state were closed for two days and everyone who could got out on skis or snowshoes or sleds or just on foot to enjoy the unexpected holiday. Andy and Kath each bought a pair last year on sale, using precious farm money, much to Charlotte's surprise. It meant that they could all go together, of course, and they made quite a group skiing through the countryside in their miscellaneous outfits, getting tangled in each other's ski poles, learning to balance downhill and climb back up, showering one another with snow.

While Oliver was in Washington, the other three and Skip and Deb had taken advantage of an early snowfall and skied through Estabrook Woods one night, in the frozen silence, the snow shimmering under the dark trees, the huge sky overhead shot with flecks of silver. They were making plans for a long expedition on the river later, if the ice held.

But the talk around here at lunch was of lifts and intermediate slopes, cute instructors, and which boys had signed up. It had nothing to do with Charlotte, and she shut it out.

The afternoon went too fast and not fast enough. She kept wondering what was happening at home, what they were all doing, where Oliver was, wishing she was there and glad she wasn't, wondering about the memorial service, not wanting to think about it and at the same time curious. She was ashamed of being curious, but she couldn't help herself.

In civics class she had to face Andy and in some ways it was even more difficult than facing Kath. She knew what was going on with Kath, but she wasn't sure about Andy; Oliver had raised some large doubts. Tentatively he said hello and asked her how she was. She gave him a noncommittal, "All right," and after that his conversation dried up. He wanted to say more, his feelings were all too visible in his eyes, but he wasn't sure how, and she refused to help him. She needed distance in order to hold herself together, and she was afraid of Andy. It felt like being in one of those little rooms in a horror story and noticing suddenly that the walls and ceiling and floor had begun to move inward, pressing together.

She was aware of Andy watching her and upset because he

made her feel guilty. But all she could do was hang on and tell herself that she would talk to him later, when she had sorted things out better in her own mind. He wouldn't hold it against her—Andy wasn't like that. Surely it was better to wait than to say the wrong things now, she thought.

As she walked home through the raw afternoon, she reflected that she hadn't even asked him if he was going to the service. She was angry with herself for being so cowardly, for dashing out as soon as the bell rang; she was really no better at dealing with things like this than Kath. How did you ever learn, she thought hopelessly, or were some people just born knowing?

The house was waiting when she reached it; waiting but not for her. It was familiar and strange at the same time, and she entered it hesitantly, through the front door because she didn't know whom she would find in the kitchen. Everything was unnaturally still and tidy. Mrs. Paige always kept the rooms downstairs presentably neat; the house was big enough, she said, so that if people wanted to make messes they could do so elsewhere. But that afternoon everything movable had been cleared away; surfaces were bare and gleaming. There were flowers everywhere: an enormous pink cyclamen in a pot on the hall table, chrysanthemums, carnations in the living room, and a dozen white roses on the dining table, which was opened out and covered with Grandmother DeWolfe's crocheted table cloth. Ranks of sherry glasses and coffee cups shone on the sideboard, and there was a phalanx of little silver spoons laid out that Charlotte never remembered seeing before.

Her mother and Paula were arranging quantities of food in the kitchen, dressed for the service and wearing the large, practical denim aprons favored by Mrs. Paige. "I think if we plug in the coffee urn just before we leave," she was saying, "it should be all right. Oh, Charlotte, good. Darling, you can be useful."

"How many people are coming?" She eyed the food with alarm.

"We don't know. Whoever's at the service will be invited. They won't all come, of course, they never do, but I'd much rather have too much than not enough."

"And people have been bringing things," said Paula. "I guess I hadn't realized how many friends Sam had."

"It looks like a party," said Charlotte. "Like the party after Hilary's christening. But it *isn't* a party." Both her mother and Paula looked at her and she bit her lip. She hadn't meant to sound so belligerent, but she was feeling raw.

"Why don't you go and get ready, then you can help," suggested Mrs. Paige gently. "I thought you could wear the same dress you wore last night. I pressed the skirt."

"Where's Oliver?"

"He's gone out with Amos. He'll be back soon. And your father and Eric have gone to pick up the sherry. We'll have to leave in about forty minutes. I hope Max and Jean are in time—Jean called to say there was some trouble with the sitter. If they aren't here, we'll have to go without them." She was thinking out loud as she often did.

"I'm sorry about Oliver," said Paula, not to Charlotte.

"Don't be," said Mrs. Paige matter-of-factly. "It's good for him to get away for a while, and we've got things under control."

"I was afraid that dog was going to be a real problem," said Paula, "but he's being very realistic about it—we didn't even have to discuss it with him, he'd already made arrangements to find it a home. Of course I'm sorry he can't keep the dog, but it's out of the question considering the circumstances."

"We were a little surprised when Sam agreed to keep him," said Mrs. Paige. "He's so big."

Charlotte said, "Commodore Shattuck liked Amos, once he got used to him. Amos kept him company."

"Darling—" Mrs. Paige nodded toward the back stairs and Charlotte took the hint.

She was tempted just for a moment to tell them exactly what arrangements Oliver had made for Amos—she had deliberately tried not to think much about that since yesterday —but she knew it would only make matters worse. Amos was Oliver's dog; she supposed Oliver had the right to decide what would happen to him. There were stories about old

170

people leaving instructions in their wills to have their animals put to sleep when they died—Charlotte had always thought that sad and rather beautiful.

But those had been stories about people and animals she didn't know. Raggedy, shambling Amos was real to her. Even though he'd done nothing to change her mind about animals in general, Charlotte had learned to put up with Amos because he'd become part of Oliver. He was an awful nuisance: snagging himself in your legs as you walked or skated, dropping slimy tennis balls in your lap, slobbering indiscriminately on everyone, leaving coarse gray hairs all over, knocking things off tables with his tail, running in front of your bicycle wheel. When they'd repainted the farm stand last spring, Oliver had finally had to take him home and leave him. Before his banishment, Amos had brushed against the gleaming wet walls, leaving hair stuck in the new paint, and paint stuck in his hair, and had knocked over a nearly full quart of gloss enamel, then tracked all over the cement floor. The burnt orange pawprints were still there as a reminder. They'd be there after Amos was gone. The thought made her shiver.

In her room she dressed carefully, washed her face, combed her straight dark brown hair and fastened the sides up with a silver clasp in the back. She wanted to look nice, although she wasn't sure for whom.

She went downstairs again and trimmed the crusts off little egg salad sandwiches and arranged them on plates with sprigs of parsley. Oliver hadn't come back.

Her father and Eric appeared with a case of sherry and a bottle of good scotch—for later, Eric said. Max and Jean arrived, Jean with a large pound cake and a foil-covered pan. Max looked as if he'd been taken by surprise and hastily stuffed into slacks and a tweed jacket and hadn't quite caught up with himself yet.

"Interesting effect," remarked Mr. Paige, introducing them to the Prestons. Mrs. Paige carefully said nothing.

"I know." Jean was apologetic. "I made him trim his beard, but his good suit is at the cleaners. He got gravy on the jacket."

171

"But that was Christmas dinner, wasn't it?" said Mrs. Paige.

"Yup. I keep forgetting to pick it up," said Max cheerfully. "Been there almost a month now."

"At least you got here," said Mrs. Paige.

Oliver still hadn't. The forty minutes dwindled to ten. Mrs. Paige was very calm—not necessarily a good sign as her family knew—but Paula didn't hide her agitation and kept checking her watch.

"I don't know where he can be—he *knows* what time we have to be there. I should never have let him go."

"Should we look for him?" said Max. "I could take a car—"

"He's got that damn dog with him," Paula said. "He wouldn't—?" She let the question hang and glanced at Charlotte, who said with all the conviction she could muster, "He'll come back."

At five minutes past three Oliver returned with Amos. When Paula asked him where he'd been, he said, "I had to go to the post office."

"The post office? But why *now*?"

"I needed an air mail stamp. I didn't think it would take so long, but it was important. Excuse me." And he went to put Amos on the sunporch.

Paula looked very much as if she'd like to carry the discussion further, but Eric took her off to help her into her coat.

Chapter Nineteen

AT THE CHURCH THEY WAITED IN THE PARISH HALL WITH Reverend Francks until the congregation had gathered in the chapel, then they were ushered in to sit in front. As she entered, Charlotte glimpsed rows of pale faces stretching back into the soft gloom, but she was too self-conscious to search out the ones she knew. She lowered her eyes and followed Jean into the pew. The organ twiddled quietly until they were all in place, then Reverend Francks stepped forward.

Without giving it a great deal of thought, Charlotte had been expecting a great and complex mystery, a ritual she would not understand. But it was not so at all. Like the interment, the service was straightforward and simple, composed of familiar prayers, lessons, and hymns. At one point a tall, thin man with sparse white hair and a cane limped to the pulpit and in a pinched New England accent spoke briefly about his old and much-loved friend, Sammy Shattuck. Reverend Francks said a little about the things Commodore Shattuck had done during his life in Concord. "And he was fortunate," the minister concluded, "in these last years to have the companionship of his great-nephew, Oliver. I know it meant a great deal to them both to share with one another." He looked directly at Oliver as he spoke, and Oliver, sitting straight-backed in front of Charlotte, never moved a muscle. She had suddenly to blink back tears.

The whole service lasted less than an hour. After the bene-

173

diction, the organist began again, the congregation stood, and the Prestons and the Paiges walked up the aisle to the back of the chapel and out into the gray afternoon. Thick clouds blotted up the light. In the trees toward the river, crows jeered raggedly; they gathered, then spun into the wind and dropped back again like huge flakes of ash. Charlotte lifted her head and took a deep breath, feeling her lungs stretch. She was seized with a sudden fierce desire to break away from the others and responsibility and run down the street home, to change into old clothes and spend the rest of the afternoon doing something strenuously physical and thoughtless, something to prove she was young and strong and full of life.

But of course she couldn't; she was trapped by the rules, and she was old enough to know it. So she stood meekly beside her father, with the Prestons, to greet the other people who'd come to the service. "It would be nice, I think, if you stayed with your father," Mrs. Paige said, as she and Max and Jean were about to leave. They were going back to the house to do last minute things and be ready when the guests started coming. So Charlotte resigned herself to shaking hands. She watched people emerge one by one, blinking, from the chapel, collect themselves and return to life, just as she had. Some stopped to talk, others muttered awkwardly and moved away with obvious relief.

There were many Charlotte knew: Mr. Pianka from the junior high, Doctor Culhane, several women from the library, members of the Company of Minutemen and the Independent Battery and their wives, a few of her father's trustees. There were also quite a number she didn't recognize, almost all of them elderly. The man with the cane was Arthur Hodgson, who had written the Commodore's obituary; his face was hollowed and gaunt and he leaned heavily on his stick.

Deb and Skip were there, together. They were becoming an habitual pair, reflected Charlotte. She wished she could be excused to go and talk to them, but at that moment found herself shaking hands with George Schuyler. He looked even bigger than usual in an unaccustomed dark suit and tie. They looked solemnly at each other, embarrassed by their unfamiliar roles, and didn't know what to say. Mr. Paige smoothed things by leaning across Charlotte to introduce George to Eric Preston.

Next came Andy, Kath, Dan, and Pat Schuyler. Andy looked as if he were being punished, he could hardly meet Charlotte's eyes, and Kath simply wouldn't. Charlotte couldn't bring herself to shake hands with either of them—it was too awkward. But Dan, next in line, gravely offered his hand and gave her a formal little nod as if the whole procedure was quite familiar to him. He was certainly far more at ease than Andy, Kath, or their father. Pat, coming behind him, reached out and gave Charlotte a quick little hug before following her family.

Some people had gone, but others stood about in small clumps talking to one another. Charlotte wondered how much longer they would have to stay, being polite; her feet were getting cold. The chapel must be empty—no one had come out in several minutes. But just then a young woman appeared in the doorway and, clutching her arm, a little old woman wearing white gloves. Thin, cottony hair wisped from under her round fur hat, and her black coat came down almost to her small black boots. Charlotte stared at her; she was Viola Wardlaw. She and her sister Ophelia were two of Commodore Shattuck's oldest and dearest friends. The last time Charlotte had seen her was before Christmas, when she, Oliver, and the Commodore had gone to visit with a basket of pears and an oozy wedge of brie cheese which she loved but wasn't supposed to eat. As the Commodore often said—Charlotte could hear him now—if people got only what they were supposed to have, it would be a dull, dreary world.

Viola's apartment at the home was tiny and so stuffed with furniture and objects and memories that the three of them could hardly find room to sit. She gave them lemon tea and oatmeal cookies and talked and talked. In her own surroundings she hadn't seemed so little and insubstantial, but in the harsh afternoon she made Charlotte think of a cake of glycerine soap, wearing smaller and smaller and more translucent.

The two women made their way haltingly down the steps and paused. Viola put up her hand to straighten her hat and knocked it more askew. The young woman asked her something and she shook her head. Without noticing how he got there, Charlotte saw Oliver suddenly in front of them. Viola had to look up at him; her face lifted in a smile and she reached out a white glove, which he took with his right hand. The smile faded gently, but her eyes were steady on his face.

"Excuse me," said Charlotte to her father.

"Charlotte, there you are. Good." Viola cocked her head. "I really can't be bothered standing in line. Not at my age. No one should expect it. But I did want to see you both. I was just saying to Oliver that I think Sammy's gotten a very respectable turnout, considering the day. There weren't nearly as many for Dolly Mortlake. Really quite thin, her congregation was. And it was better weather. Of course, that was Dolly. Very difficult to get along with, though I did my best. Still, I'm pleased for Sammy."

"It was a very nice service," said the young woman whose arm Viola still gripped.

Viola sniffed. "I doubt that Sammy would have cared much for it himself. All that fuss. Better just to be buried and let people get on with things. But then it doesn't matter to him, does it? This is Vicki, dears. She takes me out, to make sure I don't damage myself. She thinks I need to be reminded of things, but I don't. It makes her feel useful, so I sometimes pretend I do."

Vicki smiled good-naturedly at Oliver and Charlotte. "Just don't tell my supervisor that, Miss Wardlaw."

"How is Ophelia?" asked Oliver.

"Oh, much the same, dear. I'll tell her you asked and she might know what I'm talking about. She does still have times when her mind's quite clear. I haven't told her about Sammy. I don't think it can do her any good to know."

"We ought to have come to see you," said Charlotte, apologetic. "I didn't think—"

"Don't you worry about that." Viola patted her arm. "Den-

176

nis Culhane came. He's a very nice young man, but I do miss Doctor Johnny. He was so much more comfortable, somehow. He didn't smell as if he'd aways just washed his hands, don't you know. And Oliver called, of course."

Charlotte looked at him in surprise; he hadn't said anything about calling people. His jaw was tight and he was studying the tangle of bare shrubbery beside the steps.

"They've almost all gone," Viola went on wistfully. "I should hate to be the last."

There was a little silence; Charlotte didn't know what to say, but Vicki stepped in briskly. "Come on then, Miss Wardlaw, there's the driver. It's time to go back and have a nice cup of tea. Warm you up."

"And gingerbread." Viola brightened. "There's still a piece from Sunday. Not as good as the gingerbread *I* make, of course, but all right just the same. Now Oliver, you behave yourself, do you hear?" She fixed him with a sharp eye. "Sammy was very proud of you—yes, he was. And he was always a good judge of character. You see that you live up to his expectations of you."

For the first time Charlotte had seen that afternoon, Oliver's face lost its carefully controlled expression. Something in his eyes flickered. "I'll do what I can," he muttered. "I won't see you again before I leave. We're going tomorrow."

"Well then. Just you lean down to me. I want to kiss you goodbye, it's an old lady's privilege. I doubt that I'll still be here when you come back."

Charlotte held her breath; it was not the sort of thing Oliver did, certainly not in public. He hesitated and she thought he was going to refuse, but then he bent to Viola, only betrayed by the flush of color in his face. She kissed him soundly on the left cheek and he hastily straightened up. Viola gave them both a wicked little smile. "Nothing at all for you to be jealous of, Charlotte," she said in a pleased voice, and it was Charlotte's turn to blush. "Now, Vicki. I want to take off these boots and have my tea."

Charlotte and Oliver stood looking after them as they made their careful way through the scattering of people, toward River Street where a large green station wagon waited at the end of the walk. Vicki helped Viola in beside the driver and climbed in back and they were gone.

"Goodbye," said Oliver very softly, then went to join Paula and Eric who were shaking hands a final time with Reverend Francks and preparing to leave.

Chapter Twenty

THE REST OF THE DAY WAS A MUDDLE IN CHARLOTTE'S HEAD.
There were already lots of people at the house when they got
back, and she was immediately pressed into service passing
plates of food. Mr. Pianka accepted a tiny sandwich—it
looked like a postage stamp in his fingers—and asked what
she heard from Eliot, a good, safe question. While she answered, he continued to eat sandwiches, until she had to go
back to the kitchen for more.

Then Mrs. Caldwell, one of the museum trustees, caught
her and wanted to know what she was planning to do with
herself after high school. That was not a safe question; it was
one she hated because she didn't know the answer, and people always made her feel foolish when they asked. Deb told
her it was just something adults could think of to say to their
friends' children, it didn't mean anything, but Charlotte didn't
like it any better. Faced with Mrs. Caldwell, in a moment of
unthinking inspiration, she said, "I might apply to Radcliffe."
Mrs. Caldwell raised her thin eyebrows approvingly, and
Charlotte caught sight of Oliver across the living room, polite
and detached, listening to a short, stout, gray-haired woman,
who had a hand on his arm. His eyes met hers for an instant,
then they both looked away and Charlotte felt her skin
prickle.

"All right?" said Jean, tactfully disengaging her from Mrs.
Caldwell. "You look tired, Charlie. At least this is the end of
it, and life can go back to normal again."

Charlotte managed a watery sort of smile and nodded. Jean meant to be encouraging. This was not the time to explain why she was wrong.

Pat, Kath, and Dan Schuyler came briefly, after taking Andy and George home, Pat said, making a face. "I'm torn between thinking Andy should learn how to handle these things and sympathizing with him. Maybe he never will."

"Some people don't," agreed Deb. "It isn't easy."

Kath stood beside her mother and gazed longingly in Oliver's direction. Charlotte watched her until she couldn't stand it any longer, then she nudged Kath on her way past. "Why don't you go and talk to him? Instead of just standing there."

Kath gave her an anguished, angry look. "He's busy talking to one of the guests."

"So? You're one of the guests, too, for that matter. That's why you came, isn't it? You can't go without speaking to him." And, she added silently, he's unlikely to come and speak to you. "Look, Kath," she said reasonably, "whatever else, you're Oliver's friend and he needs his friends."

Kath's eyes searched hers for a moment, then she nodded, squared her shoulders and walked determinedly over to him. Charlotte felt a confusion of emotions, seeing them together: irritation, sympathy, sadness, affection, jealousy, and others she couldn't begin to sort out. Whatever was going on behind Oliver's mask, he at least responded to Kath. She saw him even smile once and shrug, and when Kath reached out for his hand, he gave it.

Charlotte did not talk to Kath again before the Schuylers left. She didn't want to. She and Oliver had stayed away from one another, as they had the evening before, but with so many other people around, it was not obvious. Even when the last guest had finally disappeared out of the driveway, leaving behind what Mr. Paige always referred to after parties as civilized chaos, Max and Jean and Deb and the two Prestons were still there.

"Well, that's over," said Paula. "Kit, I can't thank you enough for everything. You've been wonderful to do all this. How would you like us to organize the clean-up?"

"I suggest," said Deb, "that before we clean up, we all collapse for a while. Jean's brought an enormous lasagna and I made a spinach pie. Why don't we put them in the oven and relax?"

"And fortify ourselves, those of us who indulge, with some of the excellent scotch Eric brought," agreed Mr. Paige. "A splendid idea."

"There were more people than I had expected," said Mrs. Paige as they cleared places to sit.

"Commodore Shattuck knew lots of people," said Charlotte.

"I know he did, darling, but often the older a person gets the fewer people there are to come to his service."

"But his friends weren't only old," she pointed out.

Over plates of supper, the adult conversation turned to practical matters: the closing of the Commodore's business affairs, his estate, the disposal of his property. He had, Charlotte learned, left virtually everything in trust to Oliver, with small bequests to the library, the nursing home where Ophelia was, and the Audubon Society. That was straightforward enough. It was the house that was the problem.

"Of course we can arrange to rent it," Paula said, "but it would be simpler to sell."

"I don't want to," said Oliver flatly. "He left it to me and I don't want to sell it."

"You'll have no trouble at all finding tenants," said Mrs. Paige. "There are very few rental properties in Concord now. Everything's going condominium. And the house appears to be in good shape."

"That lawyer, Mavuso, seems like a competent enough man, wouldn't you say, Gordon? I thought we'd leave things with him to settle, said Eric. We'll go round and talk to him again tomorrow morning before we leave. Make sure everything's in order. Apparently Sam made some pretty shrewd investments, he said. He was telling me—"

"Hey, Charlotte," said Deb, "let's see if we can find all the sherry glasses—it'll be like hunting Easter eggs."

Charlotte had no trouble tearing herself away. Even though

she knew all these things needed to be discussed, she didn't like it, and she was grateful to Deb for suggesting they get busy.

"Oliver's stubborn, isn't he?" said Deb as they cleared things out of the dining room. "Of course, it's a real mistake to do things too quickly—you often wish later you hadn't. But Mother told me Paula isn't very happy about keeping the house."

"It's his, though," said Charlotte. "She can't make him sell it, can she?"

"Sure looks that way," said Deb with a grin.

Charlotte felt a small warm glow spread upwards from the pit of her stomach. Her sister looked at her consideringly, but there was no chance for them to reestablish their interrupted conversation of the day before, because in a few more minutes everyone went to work with them. Paula and Jean washed dishes, Max and Oliver dried, Charlotte, Deb, and Mrs. Paige hunted out dirty cups and glasses and put things away, and Mr. Paige and Eric rearranged the furniture.

Once the house was back in order they all said good night. Max and Jean took Deb home on their way to Cambridge, Paula and Eric drove off to the Inn. They arranged to pick Oliver up the next morning at ten-thirty. They would pay a last visit to Mr. Mavuso while Oliver took Amos to the animal hospital. He said he wanted to do that alone. Paula looked uncertain, thinking no doubt about the way he'd driven off the day before, but Eric nudged her, rather obviously, into agreeing.

"I'm sure they'll find him a good home," said Mr. Paige.

Charlotte's stomach clenched painfully.

Oliver nodded and said, "I'm sure." Then he excused himself to take Amos on a walk before going to bed.

Around her the house lay blanketed in night silence, lights turned out long since, bedroom doors closed. Charlotte lay behind hers, staring into the darkness. She was exhausted, her body ached with the accumulated tensions and emotions of each day since last Thursday, since Oliver had told her the Commodore was dead. She wondered with a surge of panic how long it would be before she would be able to sleep peacefully again.

After what seemed like hours, she could no longer stand just lying there. Her room was cold and luminous with moonlight. Perhaps if she got up and went to the bathroom, or made herself some cocoa . . . Then if she still couldn't sleep, she could distract herself with a book. Anything was better than lying there, crushed by the weight of her thoughts. Her sweat shirt robe was on the chair by the window, where she'd dropped it. Outside, the moon was just past full, a little flat on one side, but so bright in the dark sky that it eclipsed the stars around it. The world beyond her window shone back at it, streaked with shadow, full of a frosted silver light that seemed to rise out of the snow as if from a source underneath. A wind had come up, scattering the clouds, sweeping them off the night sky, leaving it clear.

She padded down the hall to the bathroom, not bothering with a light, knowing the exercise was futile. She didn't need the bathroom, and the thought of cocoa actually made her feel queasy. They were excuses, diversions, feeble attempts to solve a problem they didn't begin to touch. Growing in her was a sense of Oliver, down the hall, behind Eliot's door. The awareness was stronger than it had been at any time earlier in the day when they had actually been together. Suddenly and clearly she realized she couldn't let him go the way things were between them. What hadn't been said would shortly never be said, and what had would push them apart like tree roots burrowing into the crack in a ledge, forcing it wider and wider. None of this was anyone's fault; it was what had happened. But she had to confront the situation and deal with it, or she would not forgive herself.

Taking hold of her courage, she tiptoed out of the bathroom and along the hall to Eliot's room, at the far end. A thin line of light showed beneath the door—she had known he wouldn't be asleep. Very softly she knocked. Her heart beat against her ribs as if it was struggling to get out; the noise of it filled her ears. There was no other sound. She made herself turn the knob. Shadow blurred the corners of the room; the light made a soft globe. It was Eliot's desk lamp, which

Oliver had set on the floor beside him, as he sat leaning against the bed. He was fully dressed, in the jersey, jeans, and sweater he'd worn to take Amos out, and Amos was lying against him with his head in Oliver's lap. Oliver's hand moved slowly in the coarse gray coat. Oliver's eyes were shut, but Amos's were fixed on the door. They looked straight into Charlotte's, although the dog didn't stir.

"Oliver," said Charlotte timidly, "may I come in?"

He said nothing.

She knew this was going to be hard, but she was determined. She closed the door behind her and went to sit on the other side of the lamp. The light gave his face peculiar angles, reminding her of the way he had looked when she had first known him, back in junior high. He had been private and unapproachable, wrapped like a mummy in his own life, not letting anyone see the person inside.

Little by little he had unwrapped himself during the past two and a half years. There were still things he kept sealed away, out of sight: feelings he wouldn't reveal, subjects he refused to discuss, like his father and the details of his visits to Washington. But he was no longer impenetrable and aloof; he had allowed people close to him.

Charlotte hugged her knees with her robe pulled around her, watching him, unsure how to begin.

At last he sighed and opened his eyes. "What?"

"I couldn't sleep. I thought—I wondered—I'm unhappy the way things are."

"So am I, but that's beside the point. There's nothing to be done about it now."

"I mean with us."

"Oh, Charlotte. It's the same thing. I asked and you answered, and that's it. I'll send you a postcard from the Tower of London, all right?"

"No, it's not." Her eyes stung ominously.

"What do you want?" he demanded. "Do you want me to tell you it doesn't matter? I don't mind? I can't." His fingers tightened in Amos's fur. "I told you a lot of things Monday that I would never have told anyone else. I wanted you to understand—I was sure you would, so I told you the truth, not what I thought you'd want to hear."

"You told me so much, all at once," said Charlotte, "and you didn't give me any time to think about it. You scared me."

"Was I wrong to tell you how I felt? What should I have done? Waited until tomorrow morning, then shaken you by the hand and said 'Thank you very much, I had a very nice time?'" he said bitterly. Amos let out a little yip and sat up. "Sorry. I didn't mean to pull." Amos licked Oliver's face forgivingly and Charlotte's heart contracted. It was all getting worse instead of better. "For God's sake, don't cry," he said angrily. "That's useless. I just thought it would be kind of nice if I knew there was somebody somewhere I could count on, that's all."

"That's not *fair*," said Charlotte fiercely. "Even if I only loved you as a friend. You ought to know you can count on me. I don't want you to go. I'm going to miss you terribly. I *know* it isn't easy for you—it isn't easy for me, either. It hurts, Oliver."

His jaw tightened and he looked away from her, laid his face against Amos's rough shoulder.

Shifting onto her knees, she said more calmly, "It isn't the end of everything, not if we won't let it be. Truly it isn't."

There was a long silence; she could do nothing but wait, her hands clenched together, her muscles tight. At last Oliver said, very softly, "I'm scared." She didn't move. "I'm scared there won't be anything to come back to. That when I leave it will all be gone."

"Oliver . . ."

He turned back to her with a funny little wrenched smile. "People seem to get along very well without me."

She was standing at the edge of a cliff, she saw it with absolute clarity: the empty, unknown space stretching vast in front of her. And there was nothing she could do but step into it, deliberately, as bravely as she could. She reached out for Oliver, not because he could save her, but because he was already falling and because he should not fall alone. Maybe together it wouldn't be so bad. She put her arms around him and then his came up around her and they held onto one an-

185

other, there on the chilly floor of Eliot's room, in the middle of the night.

She didn't feel strong or sure of herself; she was frightened of what she'd done, but she knew she had no choice, not if Oliver was important to her. It was what he needed and what she could give, but the responsibility was overwhelming: responsibility for another person when she wasn't yet sure she was capable of taking responsibility for herself. Could that be what love was? She thought it was possible to have the responsibility without love; but could you have love without responsibility?

"My leg's gone to sleep," Oliver said at last in a muffled voice, then cleared his throat. They released each other. She saw the track of a tear down his left cheek but pretended not to, and he rubbed it away as if scratching his nose.

She sat next to him, her back to the bed frame, leaning her shoulder against his, and he took her hand. Amos lay pressed to Oliver's knee, watching them anxiously.

"Oliver," began Charlotte reluctantly, after a few minutes.

"What?" He heard the reluctance and was on his guard instantly.

She swallowed. "About Amos. It's just—well, I can't bear the idea—I mean . . ." Her voice trailed away.

"I told you. He's my dog," said Oliver. "But you don't have to worry. I'm not going to do it."

The relief she felt was greater than she could ever have imagined. She stared at the big, shaggy gray head resting heavily on Oliver's thigh and felt tears again. "What will you do?"

"I'll take him to the hospital tomorrow and do what everyone expects me to—leave him for them to find him a home."

"I thought—maybe she—they'd let you keep him."

He shook his head. "I haven't even asked. I can't take him to London with me—it's impossible. He deserves something better than that. You know—" He stopped abruptly.

"What?"

"Nothing."

She tightened her hand in his. "Would you leave him with me?"

He looked at her in genuine surprise. "With you? But you don't—you've never liked him that much."

"I've gotten used to him."

"That's not enough," he said bluntly. "He needs someone to love him." He took a deep breath. "Dr. Russell will find someone. That's partly what I was afraid of, you know. He'd find Amos a family who'd really love him, and Amos would love them, and—"

"I'd love him because he's yours," said Charlotte. She reached across Oliver and gingerly patted Amos's rough head. He rolled his eyes at her and his tail thumped the floor very softly. "And if that's all right with you, we'll be here when you come back again. Is that enough of a promise?"

Oliver met her eyes. "It has to be," he said.